SAM
and His
Brother
LEN

───────────────────

S A M
and His
Brother
L E N

by
John Manderino

Academy
Chicago
Publishers

Published in 1994 by
Academy Chicago Publishers
363 West Erie Street
Chicago, Illinois 60610

Printed and Bound in the USA

Library of Congress Cataloging-in-Publication Data
Manderino, John.
  Sam and his brother Len / by John Manderino.
      p.   cm.
  ISBN 0-89733-407-8: $19.95
  1. Brothers–United States–Fiction. 2. Family–United States–Fiction.
     I. Title.
  PS3563.A46387S26 1994
  813'.54–dc20   94-9992
                                     CIP

To Marie

CONTENTS

S A M
and   His
Brother
L E N

1
SARGE AND THE KID

I'm gonna take a look."

"Me, too."

"No. Stay down." Sam carefully got to his knees, curled his fingers like binoculars, and scanned the area.

"Damn," he said quietly.

"Bad?" Len asked.

Sam dropped back down. "Crawling with Japs."

Len moaned.

"Take it easy, kid."

Sam had seen a lot of war and wore his plastic helmet tilted casually back, the straps hanging loose. Len wore his helmet low and fastened tightly.

"I'm scared, Sarge."

"I know, kid. But we got a job to do."

They were all that remained of their platoon, but their mission was still the same: to wipe out every yellow, slit-eyed, buck-toothed little banshee they could find among the weeds and mounds and ditches of the vacant lot down the street from their house.

"Now listen," Sam whispered, "when I say, 'Gung-ho,' we attack. Run in a zig-zag, dodge the bullets. Keep thinking: 'I'm a Marine. I can do it.'" He spat. "Questions?"

Len buried his face in his arms. "I can't go out there, Sarge! I can't! I can't! I —"

"Dammit, soldier, get a hold of yourself," Sam ordered, and gave him a good hard jab in the shoulder.

Len sprang to his knees. "Thanks a lot, Sam," he whined, holding his shoulder, "you jerk."

"Oh, I didn't even hurt you."

"No, you just practically broke my arm!"

"All right, I'm sorry. Come on. Get down."

"Well, just don't be *hittin'* me."

"I won't. Come on. Get down and check your ammo."

Len sighed and dropped back down. "Ammo okay," he said wearily.

Sam looked at him. "Len, you gonna play or be a baby?"

"Well, you practically broke my *arm*, Sam."

"And I said I'm sorry! Now check your ammo, soldier."

Len's stick, like Sam's, was a Thompson submachine gun, with a butter knife taped below the muzzle. He gave the stick a shake to hear how many rounds were left.

"Ammo okay, Sarge."

"All right. Now, one more time: What are we fighting for?"

"For God, and our country, and . . . I forget."

"Peace in the world. Try it again. What are we fighting for?"

"For God and our country and peace in the world."

"Ready?"

"Ready, Sarge."

"Good luck, kid."

"Good luck to you, too, Sarge."

"Thanks, kid."

"You're welcome, Sarge."

"Gung-ho!" shouted Sam, and scrambled to his feet.

"Gung-ho!" cried Len, and followed him out.

Zig-zagging through the sunny field, their guns going *Budda-dudda-dow, budda-dudda-dow,* they blew Jap after Jap into mush. Some, refusing to die, got a slick bayonet in the belly, quickly in and out, or a gun butt straight through the bridge of the nose, brain matter leaping from ears. It was hell, but they did it. They had to.

"Over here!" hollered Sam, throwing himself behind an abandoned tire.

Len delivered one more spray of lead through a group in a ditch still wiggling a little, and started racing over.

"Hit the dirt!" Sam yelled.

Len threw himself to the ground.

"Crawl!" Sam ordered.

Len crawled on his belly the rest of the way, Sam keeping him covered.

"Nice going, kid."

"Thanks, Sarge."

"You looked good out there."

"You too, Sarge."

"Now listen. We got 'em all, except for that machine gun nest behind the bunker, other side of the field. See 'em there?"

"See 'em, Sarge."

Sam spat. "I'm gonna make a try for it. Stay here and cover me. Questions?"

"Let me go with you, Sarge."

"No. Too dangerous."

"I'll be all right."

"Can't let you."

"Sarge, come on."

"Sorry, kid."

"Then I quit."

Sam sighed. "All right, we'll both go."

"Ready, Sarge?"

"Will you wait? I haven't even said the plan."

"Right. What's the plan?"

"You go left, I'll go right, run in a zig-zag. Ready?"

"Gung-ho!" Len hollered, getting up.

"Down, you fool!"

Len got down. "What's the matter, Sarge?"

Sam pointed a finger in his face. "Don't . . . you . . . *ever* go out there first. You hear me, kid?"

"Hear you, Sarge."

"What're you trying to be, a hero?"

"No, Sarge."

"All right. Let's kill some Japs. You ready?"

"Ready."

"Gung-ho!"

"Gung-ho!"

They clambered to their feet and opened fire. Sam ran in a zig-zag, Len raced past him.

"Zig-zag!" Sam shouted, and stopped running.

Len continued straight for the bunker, blasting away, dodging bullets with his head.

Sam hollered, "Hit the dirt!"

Len kept going.

"Aaaah!" Sam cried at the top of his voice, clutching his heart. "I'm hit!"

Len looked back, slowing to a trot.

Sam stood there weaving in place, eyes half-closed.

Len stopped.

Sam dropped his gun and sank to his knees.

"Sarge!" cried Len, and came running back to him. "Sarge,

you *okay?*"

Sam managed a tight smile. "Looks like ... this is. . . it, kid."

Len dropped to his knees and put a hand on Sam's shoulder. "I'll get 'em for you, Sarge. I'll get every lousy, stinking —"

"No, Len. You die too."

Len sat back on his heels. "Come on, Sam. Let me get 'em. Then it's like, you died but I got 'em. For you, see?"

Sam shook his head. "Dumb. It's a whole machine gun nest. Come on, we both die and it's real sad. Go ahead. Get shot. It's real sad."

"Can't I just —"

"No."

"Then I quit."

"Then quit," said Sam, getting up.

"All right, all right, I'll die."

"Then *do* it."

Len took a deep breath and let it out. "In the back?"

"Right in the middle of the spine."

Len put a hand on Sam's shoulder again. "I'll get 'em, Sarge. I'll get every lousy —" He suddenly arched his back and dropped his gun, his eyes going wide in buck-private horror. "Sarge!" he cried. "Sarge, where *are* you?"

"Right here, kid. Take it easy."

"But it's gettin' . . . so . . . *dark.*"

"I know, kid. But listen. You been a damn good soldier. And who knows, maybe I'll be —"

"Sarge, where *are* you? I can hear you but I can't —"

"All right, kid, just . . . let me finish. You been a damn good soldier, and maybe I'll be seeing you, this very day, in Paradise. Now say, 'So long, Sarge,' and die. Go ahead."

Len stared at Sam with blind, frightened eyes, and whispered, "So . . . long . . . Sarge." Then his eyes closed, and he slowly toppled over.

"I'll get 'em for you, kid," Sam vowed, picking up his gun.

And in spite of the painful hole in his heart he was on his feet and racing in a wild zig-zag for the machine gun nest.

2
THURSDAY OF HOLY WEEK

At the sound of hard quick footsteps coming up the hallway the class fell silent and Sam looked up from his desk near the back of the room.

Sister Michael Francis closed the door behind her. "How sad," she said, standing there, sadly shaking her head. "How very sad that a group of sixth grade boys and girls cannot be left alone for five minutes without — *Jerome?*"

"Yes, Sister?"

"What are you whispering to Edward?"

"Sister . . . I was telling him to be quiet, Sister."

She closed her eyes. Sam knew what she was doing: counting to ten. When she opened her eyes again she looked calmer, and quietly addressed the class: "I wonder now. Do you think we could put our materials away without finding something to discuss with our neighbor? Do you think we could manage to do that, class?"

"Yes, Sister," Sam mumbled with the others.

"Then let's try that, shall we?" She folded her arms across her very large bosom. "I am very disappointed," she told them, "very disappointed in *all* of you."

When they'd finished putting away their arithmetic books and pencils and paper, she said to them, "Hands folded on your desks, please."

They folded their hands on their desks.

"Now, I have just spoken with Sister Veronica Martin. Sister's class will be back from Confessions shortly. We'll be going down when they return. Meanwhile," she said, bringing her long white hands together just under her mouth, "let us take this opportunity to think very carefully on our sins, on whatever sins we may have committed since our last Confession. Our *Lord* hasn't forgotten them, you may be sure. So we must try very, very hard to remember each one, no matter how small or how — What is it, Sam?"

He stood beside his desk, fixed his eyes on a point along the floor and said, "Sister, I was wondering what happens if we leave one out."

"One what, a sin?"

"Yes, Sister."

"Deliberately?"

"Yes, Sister."

"Who can answer his question? William? Be seated, Sam."

William Anderson, the tallest and smartest person in the class, stood beside his desk near the front of the room and said, "It's a mortal sin, Sister, because it's a sin against a sacrament."

She nodded. "Thank you. Be seated." She addressed them all. "To knowingly fail to mention a sin in the confessional is a sin against the sacrament of Penance." She looked towards Sam. "And that is a far worse sin than any sin you would wish to omit. 'Omit' means?"

"Leave out," Sam answered.

"Other questions?" she asked the class. There weren't, and she raised her finger: "Keep in mind, people: Tomorrow is the day Our Lord died for us, for each and every one of us here in this — Jerome and Edward, stand up."

They stood beside their desks.

"What are we doing every time we're disobedient? Every time we sin?" she asked them.

They looked at the floor.

"I'm waiting."

"I guess we're being . . . sinful?" Jerome offered, looking up.

"Sit on the floor," she said. "Both of you."

They sat on the floor next to their desks.

"Class? What are we doing every time we sin?" She looked around. "Valerie? Will you tell us please? What are we doing every time we sin?"

"Keeping Jesus on the cross, Sister."

"Would you stand and repeat that louder, please?"

Valerie stood. "Keeping Jesus on the cross, Sister," she repeated, louder.

"Thank you. Be seated. With every sin," Sister told the class, her face bright pink now, "with every sin we are driving the nails in deeper, a little bit deeper into His tender hands and —"

There was a knock at the door.

Sister opened it just enough to reveal the lean, bespectacled face of Sister Veronica Martin in the dim hallway. The two nuns whispered together, their veils nodding. Then Sister Michael Francis said, "Thank you, Sister," and closed the door. She faced them, her hand on the knob.

"Let's everyone quietly rise."

Only Michael Dolan remained in front of Sam as he stood in one of the two lines before the confessional box in the high and cool dim church, hands pressed together, trying to feel so sorry for his sin that he'd be able to tell it. He thought of

Jesus on the cross, the nails through His tender hands and feet, the crown of thorns through His tender skull, suffering all that for him — for *him* — and the way he treated Jesus back. But he couldn't concentrate enough to get the guilt of it. Then Barbara Stolowski stepped out from behind the purple curtain and Dolan walked over to it, and he was next.

Raymond Lewis poked him in the back to move up, and he stepped closer. He could hear mumbling coming from the other line's booth. Then it stopped and a much deeper mumbling came from behind the door where Father Leclair was sitting between the two booths. Then he heard the little wooden slide scrape shut, the slide from the other booth scrape open, and Dolan begin mumbling.

William Anderson came out from the other booth and held the curtain for Mary Ellen Kaiser, who nodded and walked confidently in.

Dolan was still mumbling. Then Father Leclair. Then Dolan again. Sam knew he was finishing up, saying the Act of Contrition, because he heard the little slide close and the other one open and Mary Ellen Kaiser begin.

He could leave the line right now, walk to one of the side doors, shove it open and run. He could do that, right now . . . .

Dolan stepped out from behind the curtain.

Sam stood there.

Raymond Lewis poked him in the back again and he walked forward. He drew aside the heavy curtain and stepped into the dark. He knelt on the padded kneeler, laced his fingers and waited, trying to pray: Dear Jesus . . . dear Mary . . .

He soon heard Father mumbling to Mary Ellen Kaiser, and decided to get up and leave . . . and remained kneeling.

Then the little slide in front of his face flew open and there was the dark shape of Father's tilted, listening head behind the screen.

After a moment Father said quietly, "Well?"

Sam whispered, "Bless me, Father, for I have sinned. It has been two weeks since my last confession. The sins that I remember are: I disobeyed my parents and my teacher . . . I lied many times . . . I quarrelled with my brother and my friends . . . I took the name of the Lord in vain . . ." He stopped.

Father said, "For your penance —"

"An impure and sacriligious dream," Sam added.

"Pardon me?"

"I had an impure and sacriligious dream, Father."

After a moment Father whispered, "First of all, a dream is not a sin. We cannot help —"

"I know, but I thought about it, Father. I tried not to, but then I did."

"I see. Well . . ."

"I don't know if I *meant* to think about it, Father," he explained, "but when I thought about it I knew I was thinking about it, and I didn't stop. Not right away."

"Well . . ."

"I enter*tained* the thought, Father, and then . . . I entertained it some more, I'm not sure how many times. Maybe ten, Father. I don't know."

"You said this was a sacri*ligious* thought, my son?"

"Yes, Father," he whispered. "An impure and sacriligious thought."

"Tell me this thought."

"It's about Sister Michael Francis, Father."

"And?"

There was no escape. "It was at mass — in the dream, I

mean, which I thought about."

"Go on."

"You were doing the sermon, Father, except . . . it was about long division." He paused.

"Please try to finish."

He pressed his hands over his eyes, and told it. "Sister Michael Francis . . . on the cross . . . up on the wall behind the altar . . . smiling down . . . with just a . . . like Jesus, with just a rag around her waist . . . and nothing on top." He kept his hands pressed over his eyes and waited.

"What grade is this?"

"Father?"

"How old are you, my son?"

"Eleven, Father," he answered, still covering his eyes.

Father said quietly, "These thoughts. They're part of growing up. They come and go. You mustn't . . . *dwell* upon them. Pray to Our Lady when these thoughts occur. Ask her to help you let them pass, and they will."

He uncovered his eyes, wondering if Father had understood.

"For your penance —"

"Father?"

"Yes."

"When I said 'nothing on top'? I didn't mean on her head. She had her veil on. I meant —"

"I understand, my son. Pray to Our Lady. She will help you. For your penance say one Our Father and five Hail Marys."

"Yes, Father," he answered.

"Before leaving the confessional offer up a sincere Act of Contrition, then go in peace," Father told him, and closed the little slide.

That's it? thought Sam. For a sin like that? That's it?

He closed his eyes and began the Act of Contrition: "Oh my God, I am heartily sorry for having offended Thee . . . ." And as he prayed he concentrated with all his might upon how deeply he had hurt the Lord: keeping Him on the cross . . . driving the nails in deeper . . . His long, tender hands . . . long, tender feet . . . a rag around His waist . . . huge white breasts with little pink nipples . . . .

He opened his eyes. He slumped, sitting against his heels, and waited for Father — who wouldn't be so forgiving this time: *You thought it again?* he'd say. *Already?*

Yes, Father.

What is wrong with you, my son?

I don't know, Father.

Don't you see what a sin it is? To think of Sister that way? To think of Our Lord that way?

Yes, Father, he would answer, weeping. *Father, I'm not worthy of forgiveness. Goodbye, Father.*

Wait, my son.

Yes, Father?

My son, your sin is very, very serious, but I see that you are truly sorry. And I forgive you. Christ forgives you. God the Father forgives you. Now go. Go in peace, my son. Go in peace and sin no more.

Oh, Father —

The little slide flew open and he knelt up straight. "Father," he whispered thickly, through his tears, "I thought it again."

"Pardon me?"

He swallowed hard. "About Sister Michael Francis. On the cross. I thought it again." He lowered his head and waited. He heard Father sigh.

"My son . . ."

"Yes, Father."

"My son, leave the confessional and pray to Our Lady as I told you. Will you do that?"

Sam spoke to the screen. "Father. . ."

"Will you do that please? "

"Yes, Father," he answered.

"Now go in peace," Father told him, and closed the slide.

Sam knelt there.

He wiped his eyes with one sleeve and then the other, stood up, yanked the curtain aside, and walked to the pews. He entered his place at the end of one, next to Dolan, and knelt with his arms on the backrest, his chin resting in his fist.

"About time," Dolan whispered. "What'd you do, kill somebody?"

Sam nodded.

"No, come on. What'd you do?"

Sam checked on Sister. She was up near the front, leaning into a pew, warning someone.

He looked at Dolan with narrowed eyes. "I had thoughts," he whispered. "About Sister." He moved his eyebrows up and down.

Dolan looked puzzled.

Sam whispered, "On the cross."

Dolan nodded slowly, looking more puzzled.

"With big . . . bare . . . naked . . . tits," Sam added.

Dolan sputtered and quickly buried his face in his arms on the backrest, his shoulders working.

Sam began laughing too, quietly at first, then right out loud. And even after Sister heard and was on her way over, he couldn't make himself stop.

3
LEN'S ENTERTAINING FAMILY

Sister Loretta Martin's always giving us these *fun* assign-ments, except they're never any fun, just a lot of work. Like this weekend, we have to make a family album, in a folder, with photos, and write stuff about the photos, and make the whole thing entertaining. That's what she said, "Make it entertaining."

Anyway, I'm done. I was planning to do it tomorrow night but the snow was still coming down this morning so I figured no hockey at the pond, and Eddie's mom on the phone said he still has the flu, and I was mad at Sam for messing with one of my goldfish, so I stayed in my pyjamas and got our family photos out and did the whole thing.

On the cover it goes:

My Entertaining Family
By
Leonard Rossini
Grade 4
Sister Loretta Martin
Room 108
Our Lady of Consolation Grade School
November 12, 1964

Then you open it.

For the first page I taped a picture of my grandmother and grandfather, extra credit. They're my dad's parents, except Grampa died last month. He had a heart attack in his bathtub. I didn't feel that bad about it. I only practically saw him once a year around Christmas. Same gift every year. Gloves. I don't think he liked kids. Or maybe just not me and Sam. We went to the wake, though. My mom was against it but my dad said, "You guys want to say goodbye to Grampa, don't you?" He was almost crying. I never seen my dad cry before, even almost. We said we wanted to say goodbye, heck yeah. Turned out, me and Sam had to go up by ourselves to the casket and look at him. He had pink make-up on and he wasn't breathing. He had a rosary in his hands like he was supposed to be holding it, but he wasn't. I started crying. I never seen anything like it. Sam whispered, "Let's go," and we headed back to our chairs, but Gramma grabbed me out of nowhere and practically hugged me to death against her water balloons, going, "You loved your Grampa very much, didn't you!" I guess because I was crying. Then Sam yells out, in this big weepy voice, "He was a good man!" And Gram pulls *him* in too. She kept going, "You boys . . . you boys . . . ." My mom came up and got us out of there.

Underneath the picture I wrote, *This is my grandmother and grandfather. They are my dad's parents. You can see our Christmas tree behind them. Christmas is a very entertaining time of year around our house. One of these people died last month. Can you guess? Answer is on the last page.*

I couldn't do a page for my *mom's* parents because she doesn't have any. She grew up at Saint Benedict's Orphanage in the city. She doesn't hardly ever talk about it.

Next page, I taped this real old entertaining picture of my

mom with her head through a hole in a painting that's supposed to be the rest of her in a bathing suit holding a beach ball. She's laughing really hard. She was pretty. I said, *This is my mother many years ago, just her head but you can see she is having herself a very entertaining time. Her name is Rose. Guess what she was raised by. Answer is on the last page.*

Then there's my dad on a ship in World War II in the Navy with all just water behind him. He's got his arms folded with his sleeves way up so you can see his tattoos, and this grin with a cigarette sticking out. He didn't get in any battles but you can tell he was tough, especially for kind of a little guy. He's still got his tattoos. One's an anchor for the Navy and the other one's a cobra snake. He says he got the snake when he was drunk. He doesn't like it. I do. I think it looks good. A lot better than the anchor for the Navy. Sometimes he gets mad when me and Sam talk so much about the Marines.

I put, *This is my father on a battleship in World War Two taking an entertaining break. His name is Lou. He fought for God and our country and peace in the world. Do you see the tattoo on his left arm? It's a cobra snake. Do you know what cobra snakes can do to you? Answer is on the last page.*

Then it's Sam. He came in for his other gloves and gave me a picture from his drawer he made me take last summer with our dad's instamatic camera, which we're not supposed to touch or even go in his room. It's Sam in his Little League uniform diving for a catch. The ball's almost out of the web and his eyes are popping out and his whole big mouth is open. It's on the front room rug but maybe you could think it's real because the rug is green. He said to put, "This is my brother Sam. He broke his shoulder making this catch." I was still working on the page for my dad. I told him I'd think about it. Bye.

I put, *This is my brother Sam entertaining himself on the floor. Do you know why? Answer is on the last page.*

I was still mad at him about this morning with one of my fish.

Then it's a picture of me and my best friend Eddie. He's a lot older than me but he's retarded so it doesn't seem like it. We're under the basketball net in the driveway, me holding the ball. Part of my dad is showing on the patio trying to get the grill to go. My mom said, "Grin, you baboons!" and Eddie started imitating one, all hunched and scratching his armpit and grinning with his teeth, and she took the picture. I'm not grinning at all. I don't like when Eddie acts like that with my dad around.

I said, *This is me and my best friend Eddie. He is just being entertaining here, doing a certain animal, comes from the Congo, likes bananas. Answer is on the last page.*

Then it's a little stupid, a picture of my goldfish, Mary and Bill. My mom went out and I got my dad's camera. You can *kind* of tell they're fish and one is bigger. That's Bill. They're different other ways too. Bill's a real happy-go-lucky type but Mary's kind of quiet and moody. Or maybe Sam is right, they're just a couple of goldfish. I like them, though. Sometimes I think they know it's me. I just hope Bill didn't think that was me this *morning.*

I put, *These are my goldfish, Mary and Bill. Goldfish can be very entertaining on those long snowy days. But never take one out and pet him with your finger and sing to him. That's not entertaining, not for him. Here is a trick question. Guess which fish belongs to my brother. Answer is on the last page.*

Then for the last page I put:

> *Answers*
> *grandfather*
> *nuns*
> *kill*
> *benchwarmer*
> *baboon*
> *neither*

Then you close it.

4
THE MASK

Sam's favorite sport is baseball. He's pretty good and I'm just okay. My favorite sport is hockey. I'm very good and Sam is terrible.

It bothers him a lot, me being two years younger and over twice as good a player. Sometimes I wonder why he keeps coming out there, because he gets so mad when he messes up and he messes up a lot.

This is going to sound like bragging but here's how good I am. Right now I'm ten, but when I was only eight I was already one of the best players out there, and most of those guys are in high school. They call me The Flea. It means how quick and little and good I am.

Part of the reason I'm so good is because I started skating when I was practically still a baby. I always liked to skate around, no tricks or stuff, just skate around. Sam never did like to skate. He always said it was more for girls. But then I started playing hockey and he changed his mind. Except it was kind of late because you should see him out there. He still mostly uses his stick for a crutch to keep from falling, and when somebody passes him the puck I hate to even watch.

Lately, though, he's been playing goalie, which is good because you don't have to skate that much. He brings his baseball glove and tries to catch the puck or else he blocks it with his stick or his body. He uses magazines under his pants for shin guards, like I do. And I guess you could say he does pretty good out there. Except a lot of times he gets so tensed up when somebody comes in for a shot that he slips and falls. But he usually makes it look like he meant to.

The other night, though, he took the puck right in the face, right in the mouth. He was bleeding pretty bad and I wanted us to go home, but he just held some snow on it for a while and came back in the game. By the time we got home, though, his lip was really big. He told Mom all he did was fall, because she thinks the puck just slides along the ice and if she knew it comes flying she probably wouldn't let us play. He told Dad, though. Dad thinks it's good for us to be tough about things. But then Sam told him there was this whole big pool of blood, and there wasn't, just a lot of drops.

Anyway, Dad told him not to play the next day until he got home from work because he was going to bring him something. Sam wanted to know what, but Dad said never mind. We figured it out, though. A goalie mask.

So when Dad came home the next night we were waiting for him in the kitchen with all our stuff, ready to go. He came in with his hands behind his back. Then he held out his hand, with nothing in it. Then he held out the other one, ta-daaa, a goalie mask.

Sam said, "All *right*," trying to act surprised, but he really was excited because it's a neat-looking mask, all black with holes for the eyes and a slit for the mouth, exactly like Jacques Plante of the Montreal Canadiens wears.

Dad said to Mom, "In case he falls again."

Sam put the mask on and made a couple great saves right there in the kitchen. I wanted us to get going but he said he had to use the bathroom first. He was in there for a while. He flushed the toilet before he came out, but I think I know what he was doing in there. Checking himself in the mirror to see how he looked in the mask.

Anyway, we finally started walking to the park. I wanted us to hurry because we were already probably late, but Sam just kept walking real calm and slow and steady, with the mask on, looking straight ahead. I kept walking backwards in front of him, telling him to come on, but he wouldn't. All he did was say, "Be steady, Len. Just be steady."

When we finally got there the lights were on and a game was going, at the far end, past the regular skaters. There's something about playing hockey at night under the lights. I can't even describe how great it is.

We went to the warming house and started putting on our skates. I could hardly tie mine up, I was so excited. Sam was still acting like some kind of zombie, though, so by the time I was ready to go he was only starting his other skate. I felt like just going out there and not waiting, except we have this agreement that I stay with him until we get picked. So I was almost begging him to please hurry up, but all he kept saying was that same business about being steady, being steady, in that same steady voice, inside that mask. I wanted to ask him what was going on, but I was afraid he'd start telling me in that voice and we'd never get out there.

He finally finished and we got out and started skating past the regular skaters over to the game. Here's how Sam skates. He holds his stick on the ice in front of him, leaning on it, and just kind of pushes himself along. You should see how bad his ankles wobble. They must really hurt. And he still hasn't figured out any real good way of stopping.

When we came up to the edge of the game somebody had

just scored and they were getting ready to start again.

Pete Lavinski said, "Who *is* that masked man?"

Sam was in the middle of trying to stop by putting his legs out wider but they just kept going wider and wider and he fell on his back.

"Gotta be Sam Rossini himself!" Terry Cavanaugh said.

Everybody broke up laughing and I thought oh great, here we go, because whenever Sam falls and anybody laughs he gets up real quick and tries to start a fight. Sam's a pretty good fighter on solid ground but on the ice all somebody has to do is give him a little shove and he's down. Then if they just skate away it's worse than if they beat him up.

But this time when he fell and everybody laughed he just took his time and got up again, real calm, and didn't say anything, like it didn't bother him at all. And he *looked* real calm, because all you saw was that mask.

Anyway, they let us in the game — on the same team, which is another one of me and Sam's agreements.

Schroeder was in at goal but he said he was freezing and wanted to go home, so Sam took over, and we got started.

It was a good game, pretty even sides. I was feeling quick and sharp and happy. I love playing hockey.

Sam was still acting weird, though. Usually he's pretty loud out there when he's playing goalie, doing a broadcast of the game like Lloyd Petit on TV doing the Blackhawks. Even when somebody's taking a shot on him, he'll say, "Shot! And a save!" Except if it's a shot and a goal. Then he'll just start swearing. But then the game will go on and after a while you'll hear him shouting the play-by-play again. But now he wasn't saying anything. Even when a shot would get by him for a goal he wouldn't say a word. Just real calm take the puck out of the net with his stick and slide it over to somebody and get set again.

Then there was this fight, Larry Janowski and Fred the Red Fraley out in the middle of the ice, everybody cruising around watching.

I skated back over to Sam. I said, "Hey."

He nodded.

I said, "How's it going?"

He said, "All right."

Great conversation.

I asked him if he saw who started the fight, even though I knew it was Fraley because I saw him give Janowski an elbow right in the jaw.

Sam said, "It doesn't matter who started it, Len. They shouldn't fight."

Which is a laugh because I already told you how many fights Sam is always getting into.

I said, real sarcastic, "Yeah, right, Sam."

He didn't say anything back, though. He just went on standing there, holding on to the cross post, looking out towards the fight. I was wishing he would take that stupid mask off and talk to me and quit acting so weird. He was starting to give me the creeps.

So, what I did, I asked him about his mouth, how his swollen lip was doing.

He said it was doing okay.

I said, "Let me see."

He said, "No."

I said, "Come on, Sam," and skated up closer. "Let me just see."

"*No*," he said, and moved away a little and almost fell.

I said, "Sam."

He said, "What."

Then somebody shouted at me to get over there because the fight was finished, so I had to leave.

But I could hardly keep my mind on the game. Usually I can figure out what Sam is up to.

Then the puck came to me and I was kind of slow about what to do with it, and Fraley skated right up and stole it off my stick. There wasn't anybody back on defense, just Sam in the goal, and I took off like mad. One thing I am is fast and I caught up with Fraley and tried to give him a little hip check but my stick got in front of his skate and he fell, pretty hard. He got up right away, though, and came after me. I didn't even have time to run. I just stood there saying "Okay, okay," because Fraley's not only really big but also kind of crazy.

First he shoved me down. Then he sat on my chest with his knees on my arms and started scooping up some slush, taking his time, humming a little. I knew what he was going to do. Make me eat it. I said to him, "Don't, okay?" I was pretty nervous.

Then Sam came falling down on Fraley's back.

I was almost crushed to death but he rolled right off with his arm around Fraley's neck, going, "Give? Give?" Still wearing the mask.

Fraley's face looked like it was going to pop but he couldn't say he gave because of how hard Sam was choking him. I said, "He gives, Sam! He gives!"

Sam finally let go of him and got up and stood there, as good as he could. Then Fraley got up, all coughing and holding his throat, and looked at Sam and I thought for sure he'd attack. He's a lot bigger than Sam and, like I said, sort of crazy. But all he did was say "Asshole" and skate back over to his stick. Maybe it was the way Sam looked in the mask — like he wasn't scared, or mad, or anything. And how could you go after somebody like that?

I said, "Hey, Sam." He was skating back to the net. "Thanks," I said. He held up his hand. I wanted to say something else, something more, but I had to get back. They were ready to start playing again.

It was their puck, on account of me tripping Fraley, and he brought it down. About mid-ice he passed it over to Stanwyck. Then I heard Sam:

"Stanwyck down the left wing! Gets by Lavinski! Passes across to Mitchell! Checked by Rossini! Lavinski clears! Puck taken by Fraley! Brings it back in! Keeps coming! Passes to Blanchard! Checked by Carlson! Loose puck out front! Here's Dimillo! He shoots! Fuck!"

I was glad to hear that.

We ended up winning, 21-19. Guess who scored the winning goal. Me.

5
TY COBB

There was still no score in the bottom of the sixth, the next-to-last inning in teen-league play, when Mr Crowley finally let Sam go in at second base. And after one out, a ball was hit to him, a routine grounder that he charged, bobbled, dropped, picked up and threw—the runner safe by a step.

He stood there staring up at the sky. "Son . . . of . . . a . . . *bitch!*"

"All right, Sam," Mr Crowley called from the third base dugout, "self-control, self-control!"

Sam returned to his position, shaking his head in utter disbelief, letting everyone see how rare it was for him to flub such a routine groundball or *any* damn ball hit his way. He slugged his glove. "Son of a bitch!"

As he turned around, the home plate umpire — the only ump that afternoon — was stepping out from behind the plate, mask off. "One more time, fella, and you're out of here."

"Fuck you," Sam whispered, bending over to tuck the elastic bottoms of his uniform pants back up to just below the knees, in the style of Ty Cobb, whose biography he'd been reading.

"One out, boys!" Mr Crowley hollered.

On the mound Macmillan lifted the ball and his glove above his head, brought them together, and lowered them to his belt. He looked slyly over his shoulder at the runner, then back towards the plate.

From the loose, lazy way the runner was behaving, Sam figured he was going.

Sure enough, as Macmillan lifted his leg the guy broke for second.

"Going down!" shouted Sam, and after hesitating a moment to make sure the pitch wasn't hit he hurried to cover the base. The catcher's throw was in the dirt but he caught the ball cleanly and slapped a tag across the sliding runner's shoe, then held his glove aloft to show the ump, who threw down his fist: "Runner's out!"

A few cheers and a smattering of applause came from the stands but Sam maintained a strictly-business expression as he flipped the ball back to Macmillan and returned to his position, glowing inside.

The batter flied-out to right on the next pitch, and they trotted in for the top of the seventh.

"Well done, gentlemen, well done," Mr Crowley was telling them as they entered the dugout, hitching nervously at his belt with his white, elbow-ey forearms. "Sam? Perfectly executed tag on that man."

Sam nodded.

"Lavinski! Dickinson! Rossini!" announced Mr Crowley's fat little nephew, who kept the scorebook.

"All right, men, last inning," Mr Crowley reminded them, clapping his narrow hands as he strode to the third base coach's box. "Let's . . . let's see some batsmanship!"

The bench began talking it up:

"Little hit, Ski!"

"Let's go, big guy!"

"Start it off!"

"Rally time! Rally time!"

Sam found the only helmet that didn't pinch his ears and shoved it down over his cap, selected a short, fat-handled bat from the rack, and sat alone in the shaded corner of the dugout: *Relax . . . relax . . . relax . . .*

At the plate Lavinski fouled back the first pitch and the catcher scuttled towards the backstop, dropped to his knees and caught the ball over his shoulder, his mitt held out like a pan.

"Open your eyes," sneered Mr Crowley's nephew.

Lavinski returned to the dugout, dragging his bat and shaking his head.

Sam passed him on the steps. "What'd he throw you?"

"A fucking baseball."

Sam let it ride and walked to the on-deck circle, where he knelt on one knee, bat on his shoulder — from a photo of Cobb — and narrowed his eyes at tall, tan Randy Larson out on the mound:

I know you, Larson. I know you . . .

Larson wound up slowly, came overhand with a fastball, and Dickinson swung and missed.

"All right, George," Mr Crowley called from the coach's box, "that's . . . that's the way! Good swing!"

Sam knelt there hating Larson's face: the Coppertone tan, the sun-whitened eyebrows, the mild blue eyes, the regulation nose and ears, and most of all: that trace of a smile. Smiling because he hardly had to try: baseball, football, basketball . . .

Dickinson took ball one.

. . . and women: Olivia Van Buren, the most beautiful girl in the school, the most beautiful girl Sam had ever *seen*: always tucked beside Larson in the hall between bells, smiling up into his handsome, halfwitted, beachboy face . . .

Larson came low with a curve and Dickinson checked his swing in time.

But handsome didn't matter out here, Sam reminded himself. Look at Cobb: with a face as homely as his own — big nose, big ears — but Christ what a ballplayer, what a *demon* on the field: a mean, down-and-dirty son of a bitch, with .367, the highest lifetime batting average in history.

Dickinson dropped a sudden bunt that caught the third baseman napping, no throw.

"Bravo!" shouted Mr Crowley, clapping like someone in an audience. "Bravo!"

Sam walked towards the plate.

"Hold it, Sam. Wait." Mr Crowley came trotting over on his long feet.

Sam hoped he wouldn't touch him.

Mr Crowley put his hand on Sam's shoulder and said to him, confidentially, "All right, just . . . go on up there and . . . don't be too anxious . . . no need to swing unless it's, you know, right down the middle . . . and even then . . ."

Sam knew what he was saying: *Wait for a walk.*

"All right?" Mr Crowley gave his shoulder a little squeeze.

Sam nodded, carefully pulling away from his hand.

"Good man." Mr Crowley trotted back.

Forget it, thought Sam. *No way.*

Just outside the batter's box he tucked his bat under his arm, leaned down and swiped at the dirt, and rubbed his hands together like a fly. Then he tapped clean his cleats with the head of the bat — one foot, then the other — and stepped into the box, where he pawed up a shallow trench for his back foot, stepped carefully into it, set his front foot, rapped his bat on the plate, spat, tugged at his crotch —

"All right, son," said the ump, "let's go."

Sam crouched in a right-handed version of pictures he'd studied of Cobb at the plate and looked out at Larson with calm contempt.

Larson looked in for the catcher's sign.

Sam took a calm, concentrated half-swing to show himself how calm and concentrated he was.

Larson brought his hands together at his belt, glanced at the runner on first, reared back and threw — *curveball* — Sam recognized it by the softer speed and the spin and let it go, the ball breaking low and well outside — fumbled by the catcher. Dickinson hurried into second. No throw.

"Well done!" cried Mr Crowley. "Excellent!" Then: "All right, Sam. Look at me. Sam?"

Sam looked.

Mr Crowley tugged his ear lobe, touched his nose, and ran his hand down his arm: the "take" sign, the wait-for-a-walk sign, the let-someone-in-there-who-can-hit sign.

Sam stepped out of the box for more dirt for his damp hands, thinking maybe he *should* wait for a walk, a ball-one count already. But a walk wouldn't move the runner and they needed only a run to go ahead and a base hit here could score him. *Way to go, Sammy!* they'd shout. *Way to come through!* But if he swung away after getting the "take" sign and *didn't* come through . . .

"Fella, come on, play ball," the umpire told him.

He stepped back into the box, wondering what Cobb would do. Probably wait until he had a strike on him anyway, he decided, and crouched a little deeper, offering a smaller strike zone.

Larson came next with a fastball down the middle and Sam dipped his front knee just enough as he stepped so the pitch went by him chest-high.

"*Ball*," grunted the umpire.

"He's duckin'!" the shortstop complained. "Come on!"

"He's looking for a walk," the first baseman added, with disgust.

"Just *lob* it in — he ain't gonna swing," the catcher told Larson, who nodded in agreement, with that little smile.

"Sam?" Mr Crowley called.

He didn't look.

"*Sam.*"

Larson stretched, kicked, and *did* lob it in, the pitch a little inside but Sam swung, viciously, meeting the ball near the narrow end of the bat and sending a soft line drive back to Larson, who gloved it, whipped around and fired to the shortstop covering second, Dickinson diving back . . .

"Runner's out!"

Double play, inning over. Larson's teammates whooped it up as they ran to their dugout, Larson strolling in, Sam standing there.

"Someone bring his glove please?" Mr Crowley told the bench and came walking towards the plate, shaking his head: "Sam . . . Sam . . ."

Sam dropped his bat and helmet and walked out to his second base position. He stood there with his back to the infield, hands on his hips, staring out at the blur of blue sky beyond right field, swallowing and swallowing the ball of tears in his throat.

"Yo!" The right fielder Fetterman tossed him his glove as he trotted past. Sam let it fall at his feet and remained staring out at the sky.

Fetterman stopped, and walked over. "Hey, come on, you know? It's just a game."

Sam said quietly, "Get away from me."

Macmillan struck the first batter out on three pitches, and the catcher threw the ball to the third baseman, who tossed it across to the first baseman, who tossed it to the shortstop, who tossed it to Sam, who flung it as hard as he could to the third baseman, who gave him a look and tossed it back to Macmillan.

There was no one on deck, and they waited.

Then Larson emerged, bat on his shoulder, and strolled towards the plate.

Sam spat in his glove and worked it in.

As Larson reached the batter's box, Macmillan turned his back on him, tucked his glove under his arm and began squeezing and kneading the ball in his palms, gazing out beyond center field.

Cut the bullshit and throw the ball, Sam told him silently. *Come on.*

Macmillan finally turned around, set his foot on the rubber and looked in for the catcher's sign. He shook it off . . . shook another one off . . . then another, though he had only three pitches. Then he nodded, went into his wind-up and came side-arm with a slow, obvious curve that Larson belted high and deep into left-center field.

"Mine! I got it! Mine!" the center fielder Cicconi shouted as he ran for it, glove out.

"I got it! I got it!" Dickinson insisted, racing from his left field spot.

They collided, and the ball went bounding to the fence. Sam's job here was to cover second base but he could see this was easily more than a double so he stayed where he was, looking out towards the ball but keeping Larson in the corner of his eye. And as Larson came charging by on his way to second base, Sam casually put out his foot.

Larson went flying and landed hard: "Mother . . . fucker!" He got up and hurried towards second base, pointing at Sam and hollering in at the ump, "How a*bout* it? How a*bout* it?"

People in the bleachers were on their feet and shouting. Larson's pot-bellied manager came pedaling up from the dugout and over to the ump: "Did you see it? Did you see it?" Mr Crowley came over too, his arms open in a question. Somebody from somewhere just missed Sam's ear with a stone. Larson was promising him from second base that his ass was grass. Babies were crying, dogs were barking . . . .

This is what Cobb went through, Sam kept telling himself, as he carefully smoothed the dirt at his feet. *This is exactly what Cobb went through and he loved it, old Ty. He ate it up. He loved it . . . .*

The ump finally cried "Play ball!" and slammed on his mask, closing the discussion.

"This game is being played under protest!" Larson's manager declared, and came marching back to the dugout. "And *you*, young man," he added on the way, pointing at Sam, "are a disgrace to the game. A dis*grace*."

Sam continued carefully smoothing the dirt at his feet.

The next batter was the squat little left-handed-hitting catcher called Bulldog.

"Lefty! Pullhitter!" the first baseman Lavinski shouted around.

Mr Crowley called from the dugout, "That's right, shift over, that's it!"

Sam played him well toward first and almost on the

outfield grass.

Bulldog's teammates in the dugout were on their feet:

"You're the boss, Bull!"

"Base hit wins it!"

"Big stick! Big stick!"

"Hit it to the asshole at second!"

Macmillan stretched, looked at Larson's lead-off, looked back at the plate, kicked and let go with a fastball that sailed away into the backstop.

Larson jogged into third, his teammates going wild.

"Time!" hollered Lavinski, holding up his glove, and trotted towards the mound.

Sam trotted over, too.

"All right, Mac, settle down," Lavinski told Macmillan, who nodded, head bowed. "Just keep the ball low, make him hit it on the ground. We'll do the rest. All right?"

Macmillan nodded.

"Attaboy." Lavinski slapped him on the hip with his long narrow glove and returned to first.

Sam stayed on the mound. "He's right, Mac. Just relax, keep the ball low —"

"I *heard* him, okay?"

"Attaboy." Sam trotted back, his face burning.

"Stroke it, Bulldog!" the bench continued.

"Rip city!"

"Clutch, Bull! Clutch!"

Lavinski hollered at the infield, "Pull in! Cut down the runner!"

Mr Crowley shouted, "That's it, fellas, pull in, pull in!"

"Hit wins it, Bull!"

"*Fly*ball wins it!"

"Bull, you dog! Come through!"

Macmillan wound up carefully and came side-arm with a curve that broke low and inside and Bulldog slapped a shot on the ground past Lavinski diving to his right, while Sam, playing a little deeper, dived to his left, glove arm extended — and the ball skipped into the web. He scrambled to his feet, thinking *Jesus what a grab*, and found Larson slamming on the brakes halfway to the plate.

They stood facing each other across the infield grass. Everyone was shouting.

Lavinski kept screaming orders in his ear: "Go after him! Run him back to third! Move! Move!"

So he stayed exactly where he was, his throwing arm cocked, waiting to see which direction Larson would break, while Larson crouched with that little smile, waiting to see where Sam would throw.

"Chase him back!" Lavinski ordered.

Sam returned Larson's little smile.

"*Move*, dammit!"

And it seemed to him they were smiling across at each other like this because they both knew that everyone for the moment was in their hands, going crazy, having to wait and see what they would do, these two great rivals, both of them perfectly poised . . . perfectly still . . . slightly smiling . . . kind of handsome . . .

Larson broke for home.

"Throw it, fool!"

Larson slid across the plate.

Sam threw.

6

CHRISTMAS AT THE ROSSINIS, 1967

Christmas is supposed to be about Jesus being born to save the world, I know, but I've been asking for hockey gloves ever since Thanksgiving and you know what I got? Clothes. All right, not all clothes. I did get a new hockey stick, and a puck (the puck from Sam), and the stick is a *Northland*, what a lot of the pros use, and I like it. Also, a little castle for my fish tank. And a book, *The Randy Babcock Way to Better Hockey*. But the rest was all clothes: two shirts, a sweater, and a pair of house slippers.

Sam got a lot of clothes, too, but he *wanted* clothes this year. One of the clothes he got, which he asked for, was this shiny, silky-looking robe with his initials on the pocket, S.L.R., for Sam Louis Rossini. I didn't tell him but he looks like a fool in it. Another thing he asked for and got was a portable cassette tape recorder. As soon as he got it he started recording everything. You should hear me saying, "A sweater! All right! Thanks, Mom! Thanks, Dad!"

I had a little money this year from Saturday mornings at the drug store doing their windows, so I bought my mom a beautiful, beautiful scarf, and my dad an ash tray, completely made of glass, and Sam a colored picture of the Chicago Blackhawks, suitable for framing and hanging in our room, if

47

he wants. I even had some money to buy my friend Eddie a pack of new ping-pong balls. The ones we've been using are getting like stones.

You should see, though. There were two gifts left under the tree, one with my name and one with Sam's. The one for me looked a little small for hockey gloves but I figured they were squeezed in, that's all. Sam had the tape recorder going and I already knew what I was going to say: "Hockey gloves! I don't believe it! Thanks, Mom! Thanks, Dad!"

So I pulled off the wrapping paper and opened the box and there they were: house slippers. I said, "House slippers. I don't believe it. Thanks, Mom. Thanks, Dad."

Sam goes, "Gosh, Len, those are really swell." Ever since he put the tape recorder on, that's how he was talking.

My mom said to try them on to make sure they fit, so I did and they fit okay, but I felt like saying, "Too small. Better exchange them for hockey gloves." This is embarrassing to admit but I was almost crying.

Sam goes, "Walk around in 'em, Len. See how they feel."

I said, "They feel fine, all right?"

He goes, "That's good because, you know, you can damage your feet by wearing footwear that doesn't fit properly."

My dad said, "Here you go, Properly," and tossed Sam the last package of Christmas.

He goes, "Hey! For me?" Like he didn't know.

So he opens it up and it's that stupid robe. He looked embarrassed. He should have been. A robe with your initials on it. He even turned off the tape recorder. "Hey, it's got my *initials* on it," he goes, like he didn't even ask for just exactly that. "Thanks a lot," he said, and started putting it back in the box. But my mom wanted him to try it on. So he got up and just held it in front of him and said it looked like it fit perfect.

He knew I was watching him.

"Well, put it on," she said.

"Walk around in it," I said.

He said, "I will," and started folding it again. "I'm going to," he said, and put it back in the box. "I just . . . first I just have to use the bathroom," and he left.   Sometimes I have a lot of power over Sam.

My mom said, "He doesn't like it."

I said, "Yes, he does. He likes it a lot."

Dad brought out the big cardboard box that my mom's antique lamp came in and we started throwing away all the dead wrapping paper and boxes and ribbon and little "To-From" cards. My mom put another Christmas record on, just to make it worse.

Sam finally came out of the bathroom but now it was time to hurry up if we wanted to get a pew for nine o'clock mass.

It was snowing ever since we got up and my mom wanted to walk but my dad said we'd never make it in time, so we drove. On the way there, he started going on, like he does every year, about how when *he* was a kid he was so excited if he got like even a new pair of mittens and a piece of fruit.

"And some string," Sam said.

Dad gave him a look in the rear view mirror.

"Just *kidding*, Dad. God."

My mom said at the orphanage they always got two gifts, one practical and one special, like earmuffs and a little hand puppet or something.

They do this every year: first give you gifts, then make you feel guilty about it.

It was snowing those big huge flakes, with no wind or anything, just falling, and my mom wanted us to sing a Christmas song together.

My dad said, "Well . . ."

"Just one," she said. "'Deck the Halls.' Ready? 'Deck the halls with boughs of holly,'" she sang, and then stopped.

I was pretending I couldn't stop coughing, and Sam was staying busy fastening his boots, and my dad was acting like he couldn't see very good out the window through the snow. My mom said, "Fine, I'll sing it myself." And believe it or not, she did.

We got a pew with Sam in first and then me, then my mom, and my dad at the end. The altar was decorated with flowers, and the altar boys when they finally came out were wearing their red gowns and lacy tops, and you knew this was going to be a long one.

After about a week and a half they got to the Communion and we all got up to go except for Sam, as usual. He hasn't been to Communion for about two years now. I remember my parents making a big thing about it at first, but he wouldn't explain. Whenever they'd start asking him about it, all he would do is keep shrugging his shoulders and look like he was going to start crying. They finally gave up and now it's just a regular thing: Sam doesn't go.

He's never even told *me* about why, but I'm pretty sure I know. It's because he plays with his dick at night. I hear him after he thinks I'm asleep. He starts whispering: "Ah Sam, you're so damn big, ah slam it to me, Sammy, I need it, I need it . . . " I've gotten used to it.

Anyway, the thing is, he probably feels like he can't go to confession and tell it, so he can't go to Communion. I wish I could talk to him about it but I'd be too embarrassed. It bothers me a lot, though, because I keep thinking I *should* talk to him because what if he gets killed, run over by a car or something, you know? Then he goes to Hell. And the thing is, what I want to tell him, he wouldn't have to tell Father he plays with his dick. Just say, "Father, I did an impure act with myself." That's all *I* ever say.

Anyway, after Communion, instead of the Mass going on and finishing up, Father Leclair and the altar boys went over to the seats on the side of the altar and these people up in the loft in the back of the church, who I didn't even know were there, started singing "The First Noel". I forgot about this. I sat back. My mom put her hand on my knee, just being affectionate, but it made me feel trapped. Sometimes I get like I can't even breathe. But I decided to just give up and listen.

Well, I started feeling pretty bad about being such a baby about not getting hockey gloves and here was Jesus being born in a stable on a cold winter's night that was so deep. Then they did "The Little Drummer Boy," with no gifts to bring, puh rum pum pum pum. I was feeling worse and worse. Then it was "Silent Night," and get this, I hear Sam give a sniffle and I look and he's sitting real stiff with his arms folded, looking straight ahead, with tears running right down his face.

Then he saw me looking at him and he gave me a kick with the side of his shoe, right on my ankle bone, and I couldn't help it, I gave out a real loud yelp.

Everybody looked, probably even Father Leclair and the altar boys. At least the choir kept singing. I put my head down and kept it there.

My parents didn't say a word about it until Mass was finally over and we were back in the car driving home. Then they started in.

My mom said it would be one thing if we were little kids, but for God sakes.

My dad said all we understood about Christmas was how many gifts we got.

My mom said, "Take, take, take."

My dad said people must have thought we'd wandered in from Morton.

Morton is this real slummy town next to ours.

Mom said, "What's Morton got to do with it?"

Dad said, "You know what I'm talking about."

She said, "Oh, you mean poor people."

He said, "I mean people that live off the government and let their kids beat the shit out of each other."

"Let's not get into this today," she said.

Dad said, "Fine."

"On the day we celebrate the Holy Family," she said, "who, you may have noticed, were living in a stable."

"Don't be twisting things, Rose. For one thing, the Holy Family wasn't living off other people's taxes, and Joseph wasn't sitting around the stable drinking all day while the rest of the —"

"Well, you're one to talk about drinking. My God."

"Here we go," he said. "Here we go."

They were quiet for a minute.

"Bust my butt eight hours a day and if I want a beer or two when I get home —"

"A beer or *two*?"

"Drop it, Rose. I mean it."

"What's that, a threat?"

"I'm just telling you to drop it, that's all."

My mom looked out her side window.

After we pulled into the driveway and got out of the car she said if we wanted breakfast there were eggs and bacon. "I'm going for a walk," she said, and she did.

My dad said, "Rose," but she didn't turn. We watched her walk down the sidewalk in her boots through the snow. My dad turned to me and Sam. "See what you caused?"

I did the toast and Sam did the bacon and my dad did the eggs, but the yokes broke so he scrambled them, but they burned on the bottom so he scraped them into the garbage. "See what you caused?" He put some eggs in a pan of water and turned the burner on low.

Meantime, Sam did a pretty good job with the bacon and I made a pile of toast and set the table. Then me and Sam sat there waiting for the eggs, keeping our mouths shut.

My dad got a beer and said what a merry, merry Christmas this was turning out to be. He leaned against the counter by the stove and took a big long drink, and lit a cigarette. He shook his head and said the magic of Christmas was gone nowadays. "It's all just gimme, gimme, gimme."

I could have said something because guess what ash tray he got from the shelf. The one I gave him. I kept quiet, though. He drank some more of his beer, and then he told us something kind of weird. He said when he was a kid he believed in Santa Claus until he was thirteen years old.

Sam gave a laugh through his nose and put his head down.

"Something funny, mister?" Dad asked.

Sam kept his head down. "No."

Dad said maybe they weren't so smart in those days, maybe they weren't so cool and *with* it, and snapped his fingers around. "But I'll tell you something. We knew how to appreciate the little bit that we had. And I'll tell you something else. We were *happy*." He finished his beer and went to the fridge for another one.

Me and Sam sat there across from each other, watching the bacon going cold.

Dad came back to his spot and took another couple of swigs and I guess he was feeling better now because he started telling us about Gramma bringing him and Uncle Frank downtown to see Santa Claus at one of the stores. I thought it was going to be about appreciating the magic of Christmas, but it turned out to be a good story because Uncle Frank was real little and he got so scared on Santa's lap he peed in his pants. That was funny and me and Sam laughed. It was kind of interesting too because Uncle Frank always drops by on Christmas night dressed up like Santa Claus. Anyway, my dad said Santa started swearing like an old sailor and held up Uncle Frank and yelled at Gramma, "Get this out of here!"

We laughed some more. My dad held out his hands like he was holding out a leaky bag of garbage and said it again, "Get this out of here!"

Sam wanted to know more about Dad believing in Santa Claus all the way to thirteen, but then we heard the back door. Dad dumped the rest of his beer real quick down the sink and tossed both cans in the trash. I almost felt like we were *three* brothers and here comes our mom.

We listened to her taking her boots off on the landing. My dad lit another cigarette. Then she came up the steps into the kitchen, snow on her coat, with a newspaper.

Dad said, "Ah, you bought a paper. Good."

She dumped it on the counter top. "What burned?"

My dad gave a laugh. "That's old chef Boyardee here," he said. "I burned the damn eggs."

I hate when he acts all nervous and guilty around her like that.

"You hungry?" he said. "These oughta be just about ready." And he turned off the stove.

She said no, she wasn't hungry. She seemed real tired and headed towards their bedroom, taking off her coat. She went in and closed the door.

My dad told us go ahead and eat, and followed her.

We ate and cleaned up after, being good. Then we went to the front room to get our stuff. Walking past their door I could hear my dad talking, quiet. Sam got his tape recorder and the box with his robe and I got my stick and my book and that little castle. This time past their door I could hear my mom talking, so that was good, I guess.

I got out of my church clothes and into my regulars. Sam just took off his shoes and got up on his bed and started playing back the tape he made, looking real serious, like we might have to perform it over again. I hated my voice. I sounded like such a twerp.

I put that little castle down in the bottom of my fish tank. Blackspot and Maxine — those are my goldfish — they both said, "A castle! All right! Thanks, Len!" I told them they were welcome. They said, "How was breakfast?" I took the hint and fed them. "Folks having another fight?" they said. I told them not to talk with food in their mouth.

Sam started speaking into the little microphone, real quiet and low: "I'm sitting on my bed, Christmas day. The time is approximately eleven-fifteen. My parents are in their room. My brother is talking to his goldfish. Outside, the snow keeps falling."

I sat on my bed with a roll of friction tape I keep in my drawer and started wrapping it around the blade of my new hockey stick.

Then Sam got one of his ideas. He said why don't we leave the tape recorder on and just forget about it.

I didn't get it.

He said we'll just leave it on and have a regular conversation without even thinking about it being on. Just talk like we always do, real natural, about this and that, and then afterwards remember that it's on and play it back.

I still didn't get it. "What's the point?"

He shrugged. "Just, you know, to see what we're like."

That seemed like a sickening idea. I said, "Forget it."

He turned it on and set the microphone on the little table between our beds. "Forget what, Len," he goes.

I just worked on my hockey stick.

He laid on his side with his head propped up on his hand, being natural, and gave this phoney baloney little laugh and said, "Boy, that was pretty funny in church, huh? When you gave that yell?" He gave another fake little chuckle.

I just worked on my stick. You have to wrap the tape around the blade very, very tight or you won't get hardly any lift on your shot. Plus you have to make a knob at the top of the handle for a better grip.

Sam kept trying. "Been a pretty good Christmas, though," he goes. "Wouldn't you say?"

I shook my head. I didn't mean it wasn't a good Christmas, I just meant I can't believe what a fool you are, Sam.

But he goes, "No? You don't think so? Why is that, Len? Would you like to talk about it?"

I shook my head again.

"No?" He said. "Well, all right."

I worked on my stick.

Then he goes, "Hey. You think maybe you feel that way because you didn't get any hockey gloves? I know how much you wanted a pair, and I guess it must have been kind of a disappointment for you, huh? When you didn't get 'em?"

I started a second layer of tape.

"I could kind of tell you were disappointed," he goes. "Especially when you opened the box with the slippers. I could kind of see a little tear starting to come out of your eye there."

I worked on my stick.

"Just a little bit of a tear or two."

I could have said something about him crying in church, you know? Over a Christmas carol. Except I think maybe the reason he was crying was because of Jesus being born, joy to the world, and him sitting there with all those mortal sins from beating off. Which is different from hockey gloves. So I worked on my stick.

He kept on, though. "That's how I figured you must be really disappointed," he goes, "because, gee, here you are, in eighth grade and you're crying? I figured, gee, he must be really —"

"Shut up!" I got off the bed and went over to him. "Turn it off," I told him. Sam's two years older than me and bigger but he knows I can take him any day any way when I'm really mad.

He goes, "Sure, Len, if it's too upsetting for you to talk about. I mean —"

"Turn it *off*, asshole." I don't usually swear but there wasn't any other word for him. Plus, I don't know, I guess I kind of liked saying that on the tape, especially after how twerpy I sounded on the other one he did.

Sam goes, "All right, little buddy. Just don't get so worked up, you know?"

I said in this real slow, dangerous voice, "Turn that damn thing off, and I mean *now*."

He goes, "Well, if that's how you feel."

And I go, "You're damn right that's how I feel."

And he goes, "You sure?"

And I go, "You're damn right I'm sure."

Sam shook his head and turned it off. He was right, I was being kind of repetitious.

We played it back, though, and I sounded pretty good. Right after it ended my mom opened the door and stood there, in her bathrobe, nodding her head. She didn't look too pleased. She said that sounded very nice. "Very clear," she said. The swearing, she meant.

Sam explained. "Len was supposed to be mad and I was supposed to be me. Just a scene, Ma." He pressed a button. "Here," he said, and held out the mike. "Say something. Go ahead. How you doing?"

"Fine."

"How's Dad? How's *he* doing?"

She looked kind of embarrassed. "Fine," she said, and closed up the top of her robe. "Why?"

"Just asking."

She gave a little scowl and shook her head and left.

Sam turned the recorder off. He looked at me. "Guess what I bet *they* were doing." He looked mad.

I didn't want to talk about it. I've heard them a bunch of times. I'll get up at night and pass their room on my way to the bathroom and hear them in there, my mom going, "Aw, Lou . . . aw, Lou . . . " I always feel like running in there and getting him *off* of her.

Sam played her little visit back, then slapped the machine off.

I decided to go over to Eddie's and give him his ping-pong balls, just to get out for a while.

He was excited to see me. It's just him and his mom. She's

nice but she acts too happy about me being Eddie's friend and not caring if he's retarded. She's real short and he's real tall. Every year they always get the same pitiful-looking tree. They must look for it. I gave him the ping-pong balls and he gave me a blue sweatshirt. I put it on and we went downstairs to try out the new balls. We're both very excellent players.

By the time I got back, the house smelled great. Turkey. My mom opened the oven and showed it to me. "The bird," she called it.

I showed her my sweatshirt. She liked it. She likes Eddie.

I went in to hang up my coat. Sam was on his bed, still messing with that goofy tape recorder. He was wearing his robe now, with the initials on the pocket, SLR, for Stupid-Looking Robe. He was playing back the stuff he taped while I was gone. The whole thing, he said, was called "Christmas at the Rossinis, 1967". He played back an interview he did with my mom in the kitchen. First, though, he had about two minutes of just my dad snoring on the front room couch. Then:

Sam: May I ask you a question?

Mom: All right.

Sam: Do you think it's fair that you have to do all this work by yourself while your husband is sleeping in the front room?

Mom: Well, that's an interesting question.

Sam: And your answer please?

Mom: Well, I would say . . . First of all, I would say my husband is a very hard worker at a very hard job . . .

Sam: And what does your husband do for a living?

Mom: My husband is a spot welder for the Illinois Central Railroad.

Sam: I see. So you're saying it doesn't bother you, your husband sleeping away while you're out here doing all this work by yourself.

Mom: That is correct.

Sam: Snoring away on the couch.

Mom: That is correct.

Sam: With his mouth hanging open, like some kind of —

Mom: All right, Sam.

Sam: Thank you for your comments.

Mom: You're welcome.

We didn't eat until about six. I had to say a prayer, which we do on holidays, and afterwards Sam started going, "Well, this looks really wonderful. We've got turkey, we've got mashed potatoes, we've got dressing, we've got . . . "

"Sam," my mom said, "have you got that thing on?"

"Pardon me?" He had it in his lap.

"Turn it off please."

"Ma, just forget it's even there. Really. Just —"

"Hey," my dad said.

Sam turned it off.

I was really hungry, nothing since breakfast, so I started shovelling it in. I'm pretty skinny but I eat like a pig sometimes. My mom told me to slow down and I did, a little. But then I had huge seconds of everything, and I was almost through with that and then all of a sudden my fork weighed a ton and I put it back down, feeling kind of green. I asked to be excused.

My mom wanted to know if I was all right and I said I was, but I wasn't.

I went to my room, closed the door, laid down real careful

on my bed and started moaning, "You pig . . . you pig . . . you pig . . . "

And I fell asleep.

I had a dream I was in my fish tank. I could breathe underwater, no problem. At first I thought, "I can't do this," but then I thought, "Well, I guess I can." I was with Mary and Bill, my first two goldfish. It was really nice. The water was smooth and warm and quiet and I was swimming in and out between Mary and Bill and we could talk by thinking. Bill said, "Nice, huh?" And I said, "Nice." Mary was quiet, and I knew it was because of being in love with me.

Then Sam was sticking his hand in the water trying to grab me, and then he had me and I woke up and he was shaking my shoulder.

I said, "What!"

"Take it easy, take it easy."

I sat up and got my bearings. I couldn't believe what time it was, almost ten. "What'd you wake me for?" I felt cranky. I wanted to go back to Mary and Bill.

"You were having a nightmare, Len. Crying out like a frightened child."

He always tells you that when he wakes you up for no good reason except you're asleep and he's awake and bored.

"Guess who's here," he said. He was over by the door with his hands in his robe, like a famous millionaire or something. I listened. Aunt Maria and Uncle Frank were out in the kitchen.

"Oh great," I said. "I have to pee."

"Me, too."

Prisoners.

Sam got out the cards.

We were sitting on my bed playing this complicated game

Sam invented, called Kill the King. Then Uncle Frank walked in.

"Ho! Ho! Ho!"

We both said, "Uncle Frank!" like we didn't even know he was out there, and Sam real quick went over to his bed and turned on the tape recorder. Uncle Frank didn't even notice it there. He was too drunk.

He was wearing the same old baggy Santa suit he wears every year, and he says in this big loud drunken Santa Claus voice, "I come all the way from the North Pole to see my nephews, and the bastards won't even come out and say hello."

We said hello.

"Here," he said, and started staggering around trying to get his wallet out of his Santa pants.

He gave us each a dollar. "Merry Christmas."

We said thanks.

Then he stood there between our beds trying to put his wallet back, telling us about this nursing home he visited that afternoon in his Santa suit and how he doesn't get paid but it's worth it just to see the smiles on those old people's faces. "You know what one of them said to me?" he goes. "I was telling your folks. This little old wrinkled-up ninety-year-old woman lying there in her bed — you know what she said to me?"

We said we didn't know.

"'God bless you, Santa.'" He nodded his head at both of us, looking like he might almost start crying.

I nodded my head back at him and said something like: "Gee," or something.

"And you know why she said that, fellas? 'God bless you, Santa.' You know why she said that to me?"

Sam said, "Because you sneezed?"

Uncle Frank didn't even speak. He just stood there looking at Sam with this real sad, disappointed look on his face.

Sam said, "No?"

Uncle Frank said, real quiet, "Merry Christmas, fellas," and left the room, and closed the door.

Sam turned off the recorder. "Kind of a *sensitive* Santa, wouldn't you say?"

I didn't.

"So what's *your* problem?" he goes.

I gathered up the cards.

Sam put the tape on rewind and found where Uncle Frank came in, and played it back. Then he turned it off and looked at me.

I said, "What."

He said, "Nothing."

Then he played the last part over again:

Uncle Frank: And you know why she said that, fellas? "God bless you, Santa." You know why she said that to me?

Sam: Because you sneezed?

Then a pause.

Then Sam: No?

Then Uncle Frank: Merry Christmas, fellas.

Then a pause.

Then the door closing.

Sam turned it off. "Tell me the truth," he said. He was sitting up on his bed with the tape recorder in his lap, looking down at it.

"About what."

He said, "Am I a jerk?"

I told him the truth. I said, "Sometimes."

He set the tape recorder on the little table and laid on his back with his hands behind his head.

I asked him if he wanted to play some more cards.

He said, "No."

I started reading my book, *The Andy Babcock Way to Better Hockey*, "Chapter One: The Importance of Proper Equipment." Guess what one of the things he says is very important proper equipment, on the very first page.

Uncle Frank and Aunt Maria finally left, and I went and peed, and then Sam. And then we were back at our places, me reading my book, Sam on his back looking up at the ceiling. One thing about Sam, when something's bothering him he really *stays* with it.

Then my mom put her head in the door and said, "Let's get to bed, you guys. Come on."

We started getting into our pyjamas. Sam still wasn't talking. I felt like telling him he wasn't a *complete* jerk. But then I figured let him worry about it, you know?

Then my dad opened the door and said to get dressed again and put our coats and boots and gloves on, hurry up, Uncle Frank's car is stuck in the driveway.

Sam got dressed even faster than me, right over his pyjamas.

When I got out there he was already down on his knees pulling out snow with his hands from around one of the back tires. My mom was working on the other one with the snow shovel, and my dad had Uncle Frank by the arm, putting him back in the car, Uncle Frank saying, "All right, all right, all right." He must have fell. The whole front of his Santa suit was covered with snow. Aunt Maria was behind the wheel. She always does the driving home.

Then with Sam on one side and my dad on the other and

me and my mom in the middle, we all started pushing from the rear, Sam running his legs so hard he slipped and fell, but got right back up.

Uncle Frank had his head out the window, yelling, "On, Sammy! On, Lenny! On, Rosie! On, Lou!"

We finally got them out and going, but Aunt Maria stopped the car to say thank you and they got stuck again.

We got them out easier this time, and she only honked and kept going. Uncle Frank shouted out the window, "Merry Christmas to all! And to all a good night!" I stood there waving with Sam and my dad, my dad saying how he keeps telling and telling Uncle Frank to get some damn snow tires, or at least buy some chains — and then a snowball bumped him in the shoulder. We looked, and there was my mom, bending over in the yard, packing another one.

So then it started.

My mom threw at me. I was putting one together and I ducked, no problem, the way she throws, and my dad got her right in the bosom and she let out a scream, not a serious one but me and Sam both attacked my dad and got him good, especially Sam — right in the side of the head and he meant it. But then *he* got it in the shoulder from my mom and he looked at her like saying thanks a lot, after getting my dad for her, and me and my dad got him from both sides, me in the front, Dad in the back, and Sam spread out his arms and yelled, "Right! Get the jerk! Everybody get the jerk! Come on!"

So that was the end of the snowball fight.

My mom said to brush ourselves off before we step in the house, but Sam started heading in, wearing more snow than anyone. She said, "Sam?"

My mom can say your name in a way that stops you cold.

"What," he said.

She walked over to him across the yard. "Let's clean this fellow off."

Sam stood there with his arms spread and his head hanging and let us brush him down, me and my dad and my mom, all around, front and back, until he was cleaner than *we* were.

Mom said, "There."

Sam said, "Thank you," real quiet.

Dad said he could let his arms down now.

Sam said, "Thank you," real quiet, still looking down. Then we all went in.

And that was about it for Christmas this year.

7
THE PRINCE OF DENMARK

S am's English teacher, Mr Ledbetter, had suffered a heart attack over Christmas break and wouldn't be back for the rest of the year. That, at least, was the rumor around school the morning they returned, and Sam hoped it was true.

Sure enough, as they shuffled in for sixth period, a young woman with her hair in a bun was standing behind Mr Ledbetter's desk, nodding at them and trying to smile.

When everyone at last was seated and fairly settled, she said in a small, careful voice, "As you may or may not know, Mr Ledbetter was taken ill over the holidays and won't be returning for the remainder of the school year."

She waited, patiently, for the cheering to subside, and continued, "My name is Mrs Morgan, and I will be with you for the duration."

"For the *who*?" Fred the Red Fraley asked from the back of the room.

Several people chuckled.

Mrs Morgan swallowed and managed a smile. "Duration," she said: "a period of time during which anything lasts. Other questions?"

"What's your first name?" Fraley asked.

She hesitated. "Alice," she answered.

"So can we call you Alice?"

"I would prefer you called me Mrs Morgan."

"Okay, Alice."

There was loud, prolonged laughter.

Mrs Morgan waited it out, then began taking roll.

By the end of the hour Sam was in love. He loved the loose brown locks along her temples, and the way her upper lip lifted in the middle, and her small tidy body in her skirt and blouse, and how she never raised her voice, though it sometimes shook with the effort and a red stain appeared along her throat. But most of all he loved her sad brown eyes . . . .

And as he lay in bed that night, thinking about her, he somehow felt certain, absolutely certain, that *Mister* Morgan was a huge goon with black hair on the back of his hands, and was to blame for that sadness in her eyes.

They spent the first week working from their grammar books, reviewing the various uses of the comma, semi-colon, colon, dash and hyphen. Sam found the work fascinating. All year in English he had done little more than draw pictures in his notebook (hideous faces, baseball logos, huge-breasted women), but now he took part eagerly in class, listened carefully, and did his homework. And on Friday's test, which Mrs Morgan trusted them to grade themselves, all he had to do was doctor a single answer to score a hundred. But he didn't.

"Now, for Monday," she announced, after collecting their test papers, "I want you to begin reading a play from your *Adventures in Literature* book, a very great, very famous play which I'm sure you've heard of, by William Shakespeare, titled *Hamlet, Prince of Denmark*."

As she wrote the page numbers on the board several people groaned and Fraley called out, "Nice try!"

She turned around, that red stain appearing along her throat, and seemed about to say something stern, but just then the bell rang and the class grabbed their books and crowded past her for the door.

Sam left with the others, but waited out in the hall. Then, when everyone had cleared the room, he returned to the doorway. She was erasing the chalk board. She looked tired. Quietly, he entered the room, set his books on the nearest desk . . . and stood there.

She suddenly turned around. "What is it?"

"I . . . " He tried to think. "That assignment. Is that for Monday?"

"Yes, it is."

"Thank you."

He took up his books and left the room.

After supper that evening Len wanted him to come along to the pond to play hockey under the lights, but Sam declined.

"Come on," Len urged, "we'll get in a game. Get your stuff."

Sam was sitting up in bed with his shoes off, his *Adventures in Literature* book unopened in his lap. "Nah," he said. "Go ahead. I got some reading to do."

Len looked at him carefully. "It's Friday, Sam."

"Yeah? So?"

"So . . . come *on*."

Sam said, very patiently, "Len, I have some reading to do. Can you understand that? Now go play."

Len's face stiffened. "Eat your book," he said and left the room.

Sam sighed and shook his head. Then he opened the book to Act One, Scene One of *Hamlet, Prince of Denmark.*

The language threw him at first, and he had to keep setting his finger over words like "moiety" and "calumnious" while he checked the footnotes at the bottom of the page, then returned to his place and read on, a few lines at most, till he came to the next strange word. After a while he got tired of doing that and began reading straight through. And the play came alive in his hands.

He was just finishing Act Two of Scene Three ("'Tis now the very witching time of night . . . ") when Len burst in, redfaced, skates hanging from his shoulder, stick raised in triumph.

"Eight goals for The Flea!"

Sam finished reading the play the following evening, then read the whole thing through again Sunday, and even memorized certain lines he especially liked.

"'How weary, stale, flat, and unprofitable seem to me all the uses of this world,'" he whispered to the dark above his bed Sunday night.

"What?" Len said across the room.

Sam didn't answer.

"Sam. You awake or what."

"Yes."

"What were you saying? I didn't catch that."

"Nothing. I was just thinking. Go to sleep."

"Well, tell me what you were thinking."

"Len . . . "

"No, come on. I didn't hear. Go ahead."

Sam sighed. "I was thinking how weary, stale, flat and unprofitable all the uses of the world seem to me, all right?"

"All right."

They were quiet.

"What's that from? That book you been reading?"

"No. It's just . . . the way I feel sometimes."

"Get out, that's from a book."

"All right, it's from a book! Now go to sleep, will you please? Jesus."

"I am. Quit swearing."

They were quiet.

"Hey, Sam."

"What."

"Knock-knock."

Sam sighed. "Who's there?"

Mrs Morgan began Monday's class by asking someone to summarize the play's opening scene.

"Yes. You're . . . Sam?"

"Yes."

"Well, Sam?"

"Well . . . the guards want Horatio to see the ghost, so he goes up there and the ghost appears and it looks a lot like Hamlet's dead father, so Horatio tells Hamlet about it and he goes up there the next night and it *is* his father, and the ghost tells him how Claudius, which is Hamlet's uncle, killed him in the garden with poison in his ear while he was sleeping, and that Hamlet should get revenge, and Hamlet agrees, but then —"

"All right, Sam, you're getting a little ahead, but thank you."

And so it went all period, and Tuesday's class and Wednesday's: Mrs Morgan would hardly have the question out and Sam's hand would fly up. When she finally took to ignoring his hand (and the little "ahem, ahem" noises in his throat) in order to draw the answers out of some of the others, Sam understood. He just hoped she didn't think he was trying to be a star or something. He wasn't after that. He just wanted her to see that he liked the play as much as she did, that they had something important in common, and could maybe talk about it some time, and about other things too, maybe after school, after dark, sitting in her car:

May I call you Alice?

Please do, Sam.

Alice . . . I know that you are lonely.

Oh Sam, please hold me?

Mrs Morgan spent the first ten minutes of Thursday's class quickly reviewing their discussions of the play. Then she asked them to clear their desks except for pen and paper, and wrote on the board in her slender, pretty penmanship: "Discuss: Why does Hamlet take so long to kill the King?"

There were groans.

"You have," she said, looking up at the clock above the blackboard, "exactly . . . forty-three minutes," then walked to her desk and sat down.

Sam spent a good five minutes doodling in his notebook, collecting his thoughts. Then he flipped to a fresh page and wrote at the top: *The Real Reason It Takes Hamlet So Long To Kill The King*.

> *The real reason it takes Hamlet so long to kill the king is because it's not just the king, it's everything, and it's all so fake and disgusting and stupid and pointless and boring that he ends up just wanting to kill himself with a bodkin, which means a dagger.*

But alas, he can't even do that because he thinks about it too much, such as what if it's worse after you're dead, ah, there's the rub, rub meaning the catch.

So he mostly just keeps wandering around the castle talking to himself about how terrible everything is and how he's just a rogue because all he does is wander around the castle talking to himself, while here his own father was murdered by his uncle for the throne and to get his mother and it makes him want to vomit just to think of them in bed performing the act of sexual intercourse together.

So he finally ends up going to her room and telling her what a disgusting slut she is, his own mother, and of course as you know he ends up stabbing Polonius to his death, who was hiding behind the curtain, thinking it's the king.

So Ophelia, which is Polonius's lovely daughter and Hamlet's potential girl friend, goes mentally insane and ends up just letting herself fall out of a tree into a brook and drown. All the time she was going down (which took a while because of her dress and all the weeds and flowers she was wearing) she just kept singing little songs to herself. She was an extremely fair and lovely maiden. Hamlet could not help but love such a creature, and she loved him too, even though he frequently acted rather strangely around her because of his troubled mind and scared her somewhat. Hamlet shows this great love when he jumps into her grave while they are burying her and tells her brother he would drink vinegar and eat a crocodile, which some people might think of as being insane, but love can lead a man to do far,

"Three more minutes," Mrs Morgan informed them.

far stranger things.

Because Hamlet really loved that woman He loved her

deeply. She was so pretty and sad and he should have just told her how he felt and snuck away with her and lived in the woods somewhere and forgot about his mother and the king and his father's ghost and wanting to die all the time. Because love is all that matters. The rest is garbage, sheer garbage.

The bell rang.

This is the tragedy of Hamlet, Prince of Denmark.

He signed his name with a flourish.

Sam dreamed about Mrs Morgan that night. She was drowning in the Kiwanis Park swimming pool, but at night, with no one around, and there were lily pads on the water. He jumped in to save her. But when he got there she started laughing, and he started drowning.

Mrs Morgan spent the following day's class period going over the material in their grammar books covering sentence fragments. Near the very end of the hour she passed back their essays.

Sam received a C+.

In addition to the numerous little markings within the text, she'd written at the bottom of the paper in quick, spikey red: "Some interesting observations, but lacking in overall focus."

He had hoped for something like, "Excellent! See me after class! We must talk!"

But they would talk, he decided. Today. After school. He knew her car: a yellow Volkswagen. He would wait for her there.

Sam's next class, the last period of the day, was study hall. He spent the hour considering what he should say to her. He

made notes:
   1. *About how cold out, say the air bites shrewdly.*
   2. *Small talk about the play.*
   3. *Mention how much she reminds you of Ophelia.*
   4. *Mention how much you feel like Hamlet.*
   5. *Tell her you know her husband is a jerk.*
   6. *Tell her you know how sad she is.*
   7. *Tell her you love her.*
   8. *Relax.*

He stood waiting by her car with his hands jammed in the pockets of his black ski jacket. It was cold out and gray, the wind tossing a few dry flakes of snow around. He hoped he wouldn't scare her when she saw him there — he felt a little dangerous-looking. He began whistling softly through his teeth: just a casual guy. But that made him feel even scarier and he quit. He checked his fly: okay. He checked the corners of his mouth for crud: okay. He checked around his nostrils: okay. He cupped his hands over his mouth and nose, exhaled through his mouth and quickly sniffed: okay. He raked his hands through his hair and patted the front to release a lock down his forehead. He felt the lock: okay. He put his hands back in his jacket . . . .

One after another, teachers came out, got in their cars and drove off, until only hers and a few scattered others were left. The sky had darkened a notch, and he was cold. He began hopping in place, hands in his jacket. Then the door he was keeping his eye on swung open again and he stopped.

It was her.

She came walking with her head lowered against the wind, in her tidy green coat, knit hat and mittens, her purse across her shoulder.

He waited for her to look up, but she didn't, so he called out cheerfully before she got any closer, not wanting to startle her: "Hi, Mrs Morgan!"

She looked startled. "Hello . . . Sam," she said, and walked rather carefully up to the car.

He moved away to let her stand by the door, remarking, "'The air bites shrewdly!'"

"Pardon me?"

She seemed awfully nervous.

"The air," he said, nodding around at it. "It bites pretty shrewdly."

"Oh. Yes," she said. "It does."

"From Act One," he explained. "Hamlet says it to Horatio."

"To Horatio." She nodded. "Yes."

"While they're waiting for the ghost," he added.

"Right."

"Pretty good scene," he said.

She agreed. Then: "Was there . . . something you wanted to see me about, Sam?"

He tried to look her in the eye. "Well," he said, looking her in the chin, "actually . . . actually there sort of *was*, yes."

She nodded, waited.

He addressed a button down the front of her coat: "It's about . . . well . . . " He was looking at her shoes now. "Actually . . . "

"About your paper?" she offered. "Your grade?"

He gave up. "Yeah."

"Well, Sam," she said, sounding relieved, "all I can tell you is, number one, you need to work very hard on trying to organize your —"

"I don't care about the paper," he blurted, looking up. "I don't care about that."

"I see," she said, that red stain appearing along her throat.

"You don't love him," he went on. "I'm sorry, Mrs Morgan, but let's face it, he's a jerk, and that's why you're sad all the time." He shoved his hands in his jacket pockets and looked at his shoes.

After a moment she said, "Sam . . . who's a jerk? Who are you talking about?"

"Your husband," he answered, without looking up.

Again she didn't speak for a moment. Then: "Do you . . . do you know my husband, Sam?"

He stared at his shoes. He didn't have to know him. It was in her eyes. The man was a jerk.

"Sam?"

He stared at his shoes.

"Sam, I'm just very confused here," she said, "and I'm awfully cold, and I wish you would explain what you mean by calling —"

He went to one knee, head lowered, fingers folded tightly. "Mrs Morgan," he declared to the gravel, "I love thee."

He should look up now, he realized, but he feared the disgust he might find in her face.

"Sam," she said firmly, "please get up."

He stood up slowly, and looked at her. There was no disgust in her face. There was sadness . . . that sadness. And with everything he had in his heart, looking straight in her eyes, he added, "I truly do."

Mrs Morgan seemed to hesitate a moment. Then she stepped up to him and touched his arm with her mitten — Sam closing his eyes, thinking she was possibly going to kiss him. "I am very . . . flattered," she said to him carefully. "I mean that, Sam."

She wasn't going to kiss him. She was going to do this.

"And," she continued, "I think that you're an awfully nice young — "

He put his arms around her waist and held her, his face in her hair.

"No! Sam!"

He let go.

She stepped back from him, turned and began frantically searching in her purse.

"Alice . . . " he said, standing there.

She pulled out her keys, opened the car door and climbed inside, closed the door, started the engine . . . and looked at him. She rolled down the window: "Go on home, Sam. It's all right. Just . . . go on home now." She rolled up the window and drove away.

He stood there, watching her car leave the lot.

He gave a thin, bitter smile. "Get thee to a nunnery," he whispered, and began walking home, holding on to that smile.

8
THE STORY OF
OUR LORD JESUS CHRIST

M e and Sam and Dad and Mom all watched this movie about Jesus in the den tonight. It was pretty old, in black and white, and all their mouths about a syllable behind. Good movie, though. Especially the guy who played Jesus. You don't usually think of Jesus showing a lot of emotion, but that's how this guy did Him. He even laughed in one scene, the one about suffering the little children to come unto Him. It was a nice, quiet laugh, like you'd expect. And when they nailed him onto the cross you could see from his face how much that must have hurt.

Nobody else liked the movie very much, though.

My mom said it was okay but she didn't think they should make a movie out of Jesus. Or if they do, they shouldn't show His face. She said she recognized the actor from this other movie where he plays this guy who strangles his wife to get the insurance money.

My dad said the guy was a little too feminine. He said Jesus was a very gentle person but he wasn't a sissy.

I said what about the scene where he throws the merchants out of the temple with a flog?

Dad said he swung it like a girl.

Which was kind of true.

Then Sam gave this big fake yawn, and stretched, and said he thought the performances were okay but the plot seemed pretty silly.

That got my dad. He sat right up in his Lazy-Boy. "What're you trying to be, a smart ass?"

Sam said, "I don't think so," with another big tired yawn, even though his knee was going like mad.

"What the hell you mean, 'the plot,'" Dad said.

Sam gave a shrug. "The *script*. The story line. The basic —"

I jumped in and asked Sam didn't the girl who played Salome look a lot like Hannah Sinclair? Hannah Sinclair is this girl at our school everybody calls Hand-job Hannah.

But Dad still wanted to know why Sam thought the story of Our Lord Jesus Christ was a silly story. That's how he put it: "Our Lord Jesus Christ".

Mom said, "Lou," meaning just drop it.

Dad said, "I'm just asking the kid a question."

Sam said, "Excuse me, I have to use the bathroom."

So that was that.

Dad lit a cigarette. "Eight years with the nuns."

Mom said, "See what's on five, Len."

It was Al "your pal" Peterson for Peterson Chevrolet, new and used cars, trucks and vans. "Folks, we got 'em all!"

I said, "Yes? No?"

She tossed her hand. "Leave it."

I left it and went into the kitchen — I didn't want to spoil the Jesus movie by watching something else.

I grabbed an Oreo and sat by the picture window. The moon looked like it was caught in Mrs Carpenter's birch tree. I sat there going over some of the scenes in the movie. Probably my favorite was the one where He raises Lazarus from the dead, especially when Lazarus sits up and they show Jesus's face, looking a little surprised Himself.

I grabbed another Oreo and went to the front room for this huge Bible we keep on the coffee table. I had Jesus on the brain.

Sam was there, laying on the couch with his hands behind his head staring up at the ceiling. I could tell he wasn't in the mood for anyone else being there, so I took the Bible to our bedroom and laid on my bed and looked through the New Testament at the illustrations, the ones of Jesus.

They were all pretty poor. He had His halo on and the same long, sad, boring, holy face in every picture, even where He's getting nailed.

I checked to see if there was a picture of Salome anywhere, doing her dance. But there wasn't, and I closed it, and got up and fed my fish.

9
RASKOLNIKOV

L en," Sam said across the dark between their beds.
No response.
"Hey, *Len*."
"Nnn."
"Wake up."
"I am."
"All the way."
"I am. What's the matter?"
"You were having a nightmare."
"Right."
"You were crying out like a —"
" —frightened child, I know. Thanks."
"No problem."
Len yawned. "You just get in?"
"Yeah."
"Where'd you go?"
"Walking."
"Where to?"
"Just around."
They were quiet.
"You worried about tomorrow?" Len asked.
"Possibly."

"Well? Maybe you shouldn't go. You don't have to."

"I mean, just for starters, I'll be living in a room with some jerk I don't even know."

"A homo maybe," Len added.

"Shit, don't even say that."

"Maybe you better not go, Sam."

"No, I'm going. Anyway, too bad you couldn't stick around for my last night home."

"Well, you didn't seem in the mood, you know? For company?"

"So where'd you go, Eddie's?"

"Yeah."

They were quiet.

"Mind if I say something?" Sam asked.

"What."

"I don't think you should be hanging around with Eddie anymore."

"Why not?"

"You know why not."

"Because he's retarded?"

"That's right."

"So? He's *always* been retarded."

"It was different when you were a kid. You were both about even. But now —"

"He's not really all that retarded, Sam."

"Right."

"He's not. For one thing, if you ever got to know him, he's one of the funniest people around."

"I'm sure he is."

"Funny on *pur*pose, Sam. Don't be a jerk."

"Fine. Sorry. Goodnight."

"Goodnight."

They were quiet.

"Real nice to be called a jerk, though, you know? On my last night home? Real encouraging."

"Well, that was a jerky thing to say."

They were quiet.

"He really is funny, though, Sam. I mean, his sense of *humor* is funny."

"A real wit, huh?"

"Not witty, but . . . just for example, he does these really great imitations. Like tonight, he was showing me the way his cat eats. He had it ex*a*ctly. Cracked me up."

"Cat imitations."

"He does people, too. You should see him do Fraley trying to pick a fight. Or Hannah Sinclair. That walk?"

"Does he ever do me? Tell the truth."

"Well . . . "

"All right, what's he do. Let's have it."

"It's not one of his better ones."

"What's he do, Len."

Len sighed. "Well . . . he makes this face and goes frowning around with his hands in his pockets, all hunched over, going 'Oh, oh, oh.'"

They were quiet a moment.

"And that's me."

"It's not one of his good ones, at all."

"But you two have a real good *laugh* about it, right? About sad old Sam, right?"

"Nah."

"Hey, I don't mind. I mean, hell, maybe you're right. Maybe I should try to be more like you and Eddie. Just a happy, carefree idiot, you know?"

"I'm not an idiot, Sam, and neither is he, so shut up."

"Twenty years old, Len, and the man can barely read."

"So?"

"So isn't that just a little bit slow? A little *sad*, in fact?"

"Not to him."

"Of course not to him. But I mean isn't that kind of pitiful?"

"Well . . . what's so hot about being able to read?"

"What's so hot about it?"

"Yeah."

"That's a little hard to explain, Len. I mean to someone who never reads anything but *Hockey Digest*."

"I read other stuff."

"Right. Name one book."

They were quiet.

"That one you gave me for Christmas last year. I haven't finished it yet, but —"

"You've read one chapter."

"So far."

"Oh, I see."

"Well, it was depressing. I don't want to read stuff that's just going to make you feel depressed."

"It's not supposed to make you depressed, it's supposed to . . . deepen you."

"Well, what if you don't *want* to be deep."

"Then I guess you just hang around with Eddie and laugh all the time."

"Yeah, well, at least he en*joys* things."

"And I don't, right? Sad old Sam. I forgot."

"I'm not saying that, I'm just . . . I don't know, I just think maybe if you didn't read so much of that stuff maybe you wouldn't feel like you have to be so . . . *down* all the time, you know?"

"How do you mean, '*have* to be'?"

"*I* don't know . . . "

"Like I'm just imitating Raskolnikov or something?"

"Who?"

"Raskolnikov. *Crime and Punishment.* That book you read a whole chapter of and now you're the —"

"But I could tell where it was going. He was just going to keep getting more and more depressed and end up killing himself or doing something weird and getting even more depressed. It was boring, Sam."

"Boring."

"Right."

"One of the greatest masterpieces of world literature."

"Boring, Sam."

They were quiet.

"Like *me*, right?"

"What?"

"Boring like me."

"I didn't say that."

"At least now I understand why you'd rather hang around with Eddie."

"Aw, don't get all —"

"No, really. At least now I understand."

"I'm going to sleep."

They were quiet for a while.

"Len?"

"I'm asleep."

"Let me just ask you something."

"What."

"Let me ask you this. Why do you think I'm leaving for college? Do you have any idea?"

"Nope."

"Well, I'll tell you why. To search, Len."

"Search for what."

"For the answer."

"Answer to what."

"To the ultimate question concerning Man's existence."

"What question."

"'Why'."

"I'm just asking."

"And I'm telling you: 'Why.' That's the question."

"Why what."

"Why . . . anything."

"Why not?"

Sam sighed. "Goodnight, Len."

They were quiet.

"All right," Len said. "So what're you going to do *then*?"

"How do you mean?"

"When you find it. The answer and all that. What're you going to do then?"

"Well, I guess that depends."

"On what."

"On what it turns out to be."

"Okay but what if . . . what if the answer turns out to be really bad but it's not really the answer but you just *think* it is because that's the way it always is in those gloomy books you'll be reading. You know? I don't think you should go, Sam. You're just gonna get like that guy."

"What guy."

"Rascal-something, in that book. What's his name?"

"Raskolnikov."

"Him. You're gonna get like him."

"Nah."

They were quiet.

"Want to know what he ends up doing, though? In the next chapter?"

"No. Why don't you just stay here, Sam. You could go to that new *community* college, the one by Morton. What's it called?"

"Lewis and Clark."

"You could look for the answer *there*."

"I'll be all right."

"No, you won't. I bet you're not going out for baseball there, are you."

"Probably not."

"See? Go to Lewis and Clark, Sam. I'll quit hanging around so much with Eddie all the time. We'll do stuff. Plus, here's the thing. I'm probably going to need your help with my English papers."

"Right. Like last year."

"No, I'll let you. It's just when you try to do the whole thing, that's all. You know?"

They were quiet.

"Well?" Len asked.

"Well what."

"You staying or not?"

"Not. But listen —"

"I'm asleep."

"I'll be writing to you, a lot. So write me back, all right?"

Len didn't answer.

"Anyway, thanks for . . . you know . . . trying to talk me into staying."

Len made snoring noises.

They were quiet for a while.

"So what happens in the book?" Len asked.

"What, *Crime and Punishment*?"

"You said he does something in the next chapter."

"Well . . . actually, he murders an old pawnbroker and her sister, with an ax. But that's not really what the book —"

"Goodnight."

They were quiet.

"Goodnight, Len."

10
THE COOKIE

S am had fallen asleep at a table in the library and was dreaming that he'd fallen asleep at a table in the library. He wanted to wake up, for there were other people at the table and to be asleep right in front of them seemed disgusting. But he dreamed that he woke to find himself home at the kitchen table, Len there reading the *Hockey Digest*. Sam told him about his dream. Len told him he was still asleep. He woke, very embarrassed, having drooled a little on his sleeve. He gathered his books and left the building.

The rain had stopped and there were dead, wet leaves pasted to the tree trunks and the sidewalk. The clock above Graham Hall read six twenty-five. If he ran he could make it to the dorm before the dinner line closed, but there were people on the sidewalk and they would think, *He's trying to make it to his dorm in time for dinner,* so he walked, quickly though.

He was too late — a busboy was just pulling the screen across the entrance. He turned around and walked back through the lobby to the elevators. But a large, loud group was waiting before the doors, and he turned around again and took the stairs, five flights.

His roommate wasn't in and he sighed with relief, closed the door, dropped his books on his dresser, and belly-flopped onto his bed. He turned over and lay with his arm across his forehead, gazing blankly at his roommate's day-glo styrofoam "planets" hanging by string at various heights from the ceiling. He felt tired. But when he closed his eyes he saw faces, faces, and got up and went to the window, where he lit a cigarette and looked down the five stories to the street between his and a girls' dorm.

Two girls, one tall and one short, both in overalls, were tossing a frisbee back and forth in the twilight. He smoked, tapping the ashes into his shirt pocket.

A guy in a poncho came walking up to the tall one and stood talking to her. The short one waited, lightly tossing the frisbee up and catching it awkwardly between her hands.

The phone rang. He sighed and walked over to the wall by the door, knowing who it was.

"Hello."

"Is Jerry there?" his roommate's girlfriend asked.

"No, he's not."

"Is he on the floor somewhere?"

"I don't know. I'll tell him you called, okay?"

"Well . . . "

"Bye." He hung up, but left his hand on the phone. After a moment he lifted it and dialed his parents' number, hoping Len would answer.

"Hello?" his mother said.

He didn't speak. She would think he was calling from loneliness or something.

"Hello?" she said again.

He hung up the phone and wandered back to the window. The guy in the poncho was gone and the girls were tossing the frisbee again, talking and laughing — probably about the guy in the poncho, he thought. He finished his cigarette and crushed it in the ash tray on his desk.

He decided he might as well do some work. Along with the biology test he'd been studying for in the library he had a 250 word essay due tomorrow for his Modern British Literature class, on Matthew Arnold's "Dover Beach". He switched on the light above his desk, sat and opened his book to the poem and read it over twice. Then he lit another cigarette, and wrote in his notebook:

> The poem entitled "Dover Beach," written by the famous and fairly brilliant nineteenth century English poet Matthew Arnold in the year of eighteen sixty-five, is a rather profound and quite depressing statement composed in free verse, modern for its time not only in its technical aspects, being totally unrhymed and written in quite irregular meter, but also in the bleakly negative nature of its content, expressing as it does the total, absolute meaninglessness of human existence.

He counted the words.

As he sat there considering what else to say, his stomach made a coiling noise and he remembered he hadn't eaten since breakfast: a bowl of Cheerios and a sweet roll. He was suddenly very hungry. There were junk food machines in the basement, but he didn't feel like making the trip. His stomach spoke again. He glanced at the door, got up quickly and stepped over to the shelf on the wall above his roommate's bed and opened the sliding panel: a box of Ritz crackers, a tube of Squeeze Cheeze, a plastic bag full of cupcakes and another full of chocolate chip cookies — his roommate's girl friend was a Home Economics major. He thought quickly:

Crackers and cheese would be best but he was afraid of the time it would take. The cupcakes looked good but there were only five, and one less would be noticeable. Plenty of cookies, though, and he took one, closed the panel and returned to his desk.

As he ate — in small, savoring bites — he added more words to his essay.

He was almost through with the cookie when his roommate hurried in, saying "There he is, there he is" as he headed towards the other desk. Sam looked the other way at something and slipped the last bite in his mouth, chewed quickly, and swallowed.

"Hi," he said.

"How'd you guess?" Jerry was flipping through the collection of record albums he kept in three orange crates on his desk. "Got an urgent request for Iron Butterfly, and where . . . the fuck . . . is it?"

"Whose room you in?" Sam asked, just wondering.

"Maniac's."

"With the beard?"

"Yeah. Christ, did I get zonked," bragged Jerry. "I'm back now, but man I was flying."

"Mm."

"And you know what I had? Guess. Take a guess, man."

Sam said, "I don't know," looking over the poem again.

"Grass. That's all. And I was flying!"

"Prob'ly spiked with something," Sam said, turning a page. "LSD or something."

Jerry broke into a high-pitched laugh. "Right!" He said. "Musta been!"

Sam turned around in his chair. "Sorry," he said to his roommate's long blonde pony tail. "Guess I'm not very knowledgeable about things like using drugs to . . . to . . . "

"Escape reality?"

"That's right."

Jerry laughed again and shook his head, still flipping through his albums. "Sometimes you kill me, man."

"Sometimes I'd like to," Sam said, and returned to his book, his heart banging.

After a moment Jerry came over and stood by the desk. "Hey," he said quietly.

"What," Sam answered, without looking up.

"That's a pretty intense thing to say, you know? You'd like to kill me? That's pretty intense."

"I'm an intense person," Sam said, eyes on his book.

"I've noticed that, man."

"And I wish you'd quit calling me 'man' all the time," Sam added.

"No problem," Jerry told him, calmly, quietly. "Can I say something, though?"

"What."

"You should try to mellow out a little. I'm serious, man. You should try to just —"

"You called me 'man' again."

"Hey, well, I'm sorry," Jerry said, much louder. "I'm just trying to tell you, that's all. All right?"

"All right," Sam answered, satisfied at having drawn him out of his mellow voice.

There was a pause. Sam knew what was coming.

"Hey," Jerry said, offering his hand.

Sam gave him his hand without looking up and let him maneuver it into a love and brotherhood shake. "Peace," Jerry said.

"Right."

Sam got his hand back and tried to begin reading the poem again, Jerry returning to his albums.

"Hey, I didn't finish my story. I was telling you, that pot we did? Know how we did it? Guess, man."

"I don't know," Sam said, and continued reading.

"Cookies. My chick gave me these cookies she made with the shit mixed in, right in with the batter. I ate two of 'em and ten minutes later I was floating, man, and I mean out among the fucking planets."

Sam turned around in his chair.

"*Here* it is," Jerry said, pulling out an album. He headed towards the door with it. "Catch you later."

"Jerry?"

"Yo."

"Listen . . . " He hesitated.

"Yeah?"

"Your girlfriend called."

Jerry nodded. "Thanks." He left the room, closing the door behind him.

Sam sat there a moment.

Then he suddenly got down on his knees and pulled the trash can out from under his desk, lowered his head above it and stuck his finger down his throat. He gagged. He stuck his finger deeper down his throat and gagged again, his ribs gripping. "Oh, Jesus," he whispered.

He got up and went to the door and locked it and began walking up and down the room.

"Oh, Jesus."

He noticed how heavily his hands were sweating, and the iciness at the pit of his stomach, and a sinister stillness in the room.

It's starting, he thought.

He held his hands together, fingers locked, as he marched between the door and the window, commanding himself to hold on, hold on. "Don't panic," he said aloud, and, hearing himself beginning to panic, stepped quickly over to his desk, seized the back of the chair and told himself this was *not* the marijuana making him scared, this was merely him being scared of how scared he thought the marijuana was making him, and that was stupid — "Stupid," he said aloud — because all the marijuana did was make you high, *pleasantly* high, like *floating*, you just let go and floated for a while, that's all. And he let go the chair, slowly lifted his arms out beside him, turned, and began moving around the room in slow, beautiful motion.

This, he thought, this is what it's like.

After several very slow, very graceful flights around the room, he drew up at the window, lowered his wings, and looked serenely down.

The street lights were on now, and the girls with the frisbee had been joined by the guy in the poncho and a red-haired guy in a Buffalo Bill jacket, the four of them in a wide ring, tossing the frisbee, which slid through the air, and hovered, floated lower, was caught, and tossed again.

They're stoned too, he thought, and nodded.

The short girl tried flipping the frisbee under her leg but failed, and laughed, the others laughing with her, Sam smiling. He liked these people. He liked them a lot.

Someone tried the door, then knocked.

"Coming," Sam called, and walked calmly over.

It was Jerry again.

"Jare," he said. "Hi. Come in. I forgot I locked it."

Jerry looked at him, a little suspiciously it seemed, and headed over to his desk.

"Another request?" Sam asked.

"Maniac wants his Airplane album back. I forgot I had it."

"*Jeff*erson Airplane, right?"

"Right."

Sam left the door open and strolled towards the window. "That's an interesting name. Jefferson Airplane."

Jerry glanced at him, and returned to his albums.

"Sorry about locking the door like that," Sam told him, and sat on the window sill.

"No big deal."

"But it *is*, Jare. We lock ourselves in. We . . . close the door and lock it. No trespassing!" He laughed. "Right?"

"Guess so," Jerry answered, flipping quicker through his albums.

"Actually," Sam went on, "the reason I locked it, I got a little . . . well, a little panic-stricken, I suppose you could call it."

"Oh?"

"Just for a couple of minutes. Anyway, I guess I might as well tell you, Jare. I ate one of those cookies of yours."

"Man," laughed Jerry, seeming relieved as he turned to Sam, "no reason to *panic*."

"I know," Sam said. "I know that now."

"For real. Help yourself," Jerry said, and turned back to his crates.

"Well, thanks," Sam told him. "I appreciate the offer. But I think . . . I really think just this once was all I needed."

Jerry nodded, pulling out an album. "Pretty bad, huh?"

"At first," Sam said. "But then, what I did, I just let go. You know? I just . . . let it *take* me. Know what I mean?"

"Not exactly, man."

"I just went like this," Sam said, closing his eyes. "Just

very, very slowly lifted my arms out, then very, very —"

"Can I say something?"

Sam opened his eyes. "Sure," he said, still holding out his arms.

"I don't know if you're trying to freak me out or something but you're doing a pretty good job, man, okay?"

Sam dropped his arms. "Jare, I've never been so serious in my life."

Jerry said quietly, "Wow."

"'Wow' is right. But let me ask you something."

"I better get back with this," Jerry said, holding up the album.

"All right, but let me just ask you."

"What."

"The first time *you* took marijuana? I'm just wondering. After you came down? Did you *stay* different? — I mean, from the way you were before you took it. Or do you have to keep —"

"Hold it, man, wait, wait."

"Sure."

"Were you getting *high* in here?"

"I *told* you, Jare. I ate one of your cookies!"

Jerry shook his head as if to clear it, then walked with three long strides to his shelf and opened the panel. "You're talking about these, right?"

Sam nodded. "I should've asked. I thought they were just regular cookies, but I still should've . . . What's so funny?"

Jerry sat down on the edge of his bed laughing and shaking his head at the floor.

"How about sharing this with me, Jare."

Jerry looked at him. "Nothing in *those* cookies, man, except . . . chocolate chips," he managed to say, and broke out laughing again.

Sam sat there.

Jerry stopped himself. "Sorry," he said, wiping his eyes. "It's just . . . kind of funny, you know? Don't you think?"

Sam didn't say.

Jerry coughed. "Anyway . . . " He stood up. "I better get back. So —" he almost began laughing again — "catch you later, man."

Sam followed him towards the doorway. "You're going to tell them all about it, aren't you."

Jerry turned.

"Aren't you," Sam repeated.

Jerry said quietly, "Hey. This is between you and me, man," and held out his hand.

Sam looked at it.

"Right?" Jerry added.

Sam gave up his hand and let him shift it around once again into a peace, love and brotherhood shake.

"Later," Jerry said, and headed down the hallway with the Jefferson Airplane album and his funny story.

Sam closed the door.

He stuck his hands in his pockets and wandered back to the window.

The frisbee people were sitting on the steps to the girls' dorm now, talking together, laughing . . . .

He went back to the door and locked it and switched off the overhead light. Returning, he switched off his desk light, switched off Jerry's, and stood in the middle of the room. Slowly, with all his concentration, he lifted his arms out beside him. Then he turned — slowly, beautifully — and began moving around in the dark.

11
LEN AND DORIS

I don't know what to do. There's this girl at school that I think is in love with me or something. Her name is Doris and she keeps coming up to me in the hallway or in the cafeteria or outside by the buses, going "Well, he*llo* there."

She tells me about her classes, about getting her driver's license soon, about having to put her cat to sleep, about being left-handed. Or she'll ask me stuff, personal stuff, like my religion or if I ever had mono. Or she'll even ask me if I like a certain thing she's wearing that day. Like last week, she wanted to know if I liked this red sweater she had on. I said it was okay. She said it was a birthday present from her brother. I said, "Oh." She said her brother's in the Coast Guard. I said, "Oh." Which is about all I ever say to her but she doesn't even mind, she just keeps telling me how *she* used to be shy once, too. Which I'm not, at all.

And the thing is, people are starting to think we're *going* with each other, and I hate to say this but she's pretty homely. For one thing, her nose is about as big as Sam's. I'm not kidding.

Like the other day, this friend of mine Bill Wiggins comes up to my locker and goes, "Hey, how's your woman?"

I told him, "She's not my woman, okay?"

"Right," he said. "What's her name, Fido?"

I said, "No, it's Rover," just to show him she's not my woman. But then as soon as I said it I felt horrible. And then, when he said I better be careful because she might have rabies, I shoved him in the chest and yelled, "Shut up!"

He looked at me like I was crazy. I felt like it, too. Good thing a hall guard was there.

Anyway, I don't know what to do. I even wrote to Sam about her. He wrote back right away and told me not to think of her as a girl but as a human being crying out for companionship. I didn't like that idea at all. It made me feel like if I finally told her to leave me alone she'd kill herself. Or maybe not *kill* herself, but go back to being like a little mouse. She told me she used to go around school like a little mouse, always keeping to the walls. Which is kind of interesting.

The thing is, sometimes she can be kind of interesting, some of the stuff she talks about.

In fact, she probably wouldn't be all that bad to talk to if there wasn't anybody around to see us and think we're going with each other. For example, if we met somewhere after dark, say the first base dugout in Parker Field. I probably wouldn't mind that. I probably wouldn't even mind answering some of the questions she keeps asking me about myself. I'd probably end up telling her a lot, in fact. Stuff I wouldn't even tell Sam. Sometimes I even think about how it would be if she wanted to hold hands while we sat there talking.

But I know that's just feeling desperate because this is my junior year and I still haven't even been out with anyone. Except, the thing is, I'm not really desperate. There's this girl Jennifer Layton I've had my eye on for quite some time now. So far I haven't seen her with anyone who looks like he must be her boyfriend, but I better move soon because you should see her. She's not only extremely pretty but every little thing she *does* is pretty, even just coughing. She had this real bad cough about a month ago. She had it for a whole week. I started bringing cough drops with me, but did I go up to her and say, "Excuse me, Jennifer, would you care for a cough drop?" No, I did not.

Actually, I've never even said hello to her yet and I probably never will and in fact I keep hoping to see her with somebody who looks like he must be her boyfriend so I can give up and relax. That's the thing about these thoughts I keep sometimes having about this girl Doris — I mean about meeting her somewhere after dark. I'm very relaxed with her in these thoughts, sitting there talking, holding hands. I just wish she wasn't so homely.

But then I guess she wouldn't be after somebody like me, right?

Anyway, here's the thing. The last time she stopped me today, on my way to the buses, I ended up saying a few things back to her, instead of just "Oh" or whatever. It was getting real cloudy out, real fast, and she asked me if I thought it was going to rain, and I said, "I don't know." Which is all I would usually say. But then I said, "Looks like it."

And she said, "Gosh, I hope not."

And I said, "Me, neither."

So all of a sudden, there we were, having this regular back-and-forth conversation.

"But, you know," she said, "sometimes it's kind of nice when it rains."

And I said, "As long as you're not *out* in it."

She threw her whole head back and laughed and said, "Right!"

It wasn't that funny. She was just being encouraging.

Then I saw my bus coming, good old 4B, and I told her I had to go.

She put her hand right on my arm and said, real serious, looking me dead in the eye, "See you tomorrow, Leonard."

I said, "Okay." I just wanted to get out of there.

So now she probably thinks I'm finally coming around. In fact, I have this very queasy feeling she's thinking about me right now, in her room, listening to The Bee Gees, her favorite group. Tomorrow she'll probably wear that sweater I told her was okay.

I don't know what to do.

12

THE MOVEMENT

Dear Len,
How's it going? Playing much hockey? How's school? How's Mrs Morgan? You still going out with that girl Doris?

I'm doing okay. Life in the dorm is about the same as I told you over Christmas, about the guys on this floor and their little groups. My roommate is still friendly as ever when we're in the room together, but I know damn well he talks about me when he's with his drugged-up buddies. I don't know what he says, but I'm sure that's why he's so friendly. Guilt.

Most of my classes this semester are good, especially one called Contemporary Moral Issues with this guy Dr Zimmerman. You should see him, Len. He's just this very tall, skinny, mostly baldheaded, extremely hyper guy with a band-aid holding the stem of his glasses. What a teacher, though. Half the time he doesn't even bother taking roll but just drops his briefcase on his desk and starts walking all over the front of the room, talking 95 miles an hour and running his hand over his head like there was hair there. Everybody hunches over their desk scribbling away trying to keep up with him but I just sit back and listen. You should hear some of the stuff he comes out with. When I get home for Easter I'll fill you in on the <u>real</u> story behind the war in Vietnam. You'll shit.

My roommate just laughed in his sleep. I feel like waking him up and making sure it wasn't about me.

Well, that's it for now. Take it easy, Len. Write to me.

Sam

P.S. How's Mom and Dad? Say hi.

Dear Sam,

First I'll answer your questions.

About hockey, I've been playing a lot but there's this new guy working at the park and he keeps bugging us about leaving more room for the regular skaters so we're practically just in this one little corner.

About school, it's okay. Mrs Morgan asked me the other day how you were. I said good. She's really nice. Not much control over the class though.

About Doris, we're not going together anymore. She told me she needed room to breathe. I told her go ahead and breathe, I don't care. I don't, either. Maybe a little.

Hey Sam, about those guys on the floor, maybe you should try to get to know them better. They can't all be jerks. Plus, maybe your roommate is friendly because he likes you, you know?

Mom and Dad are fine.

Well, bye.

Len

Dear Len,

How's it going? Sorry about Doris. Want some advice? Don't depend on people.

Well, I wish you could have been in my Contemporary Moral Issues class today. We each had to bring something that represented an example of a politically-motivated distortion of the truth and talk about it in front of the class. Most people brought newspaper articles but you know what I brought? A banana. That's right, a banana. I volunteered to be the first one up. I wasn't even all that nervous. First, I held up the banana, not saying anything. A couple people laughed. Fine. I waited. Then, very calmly, I pointed out the label on the banana, which was for the Chiquita Banana Company with that little drawing of a banana dressed up like a native woman, smiling all happy and gay — which I said was a distortion because the people in those little countries down there work for American companies that have come in and robbed them of their natural, happy native culture and turned them almost into slaves because we hardly have to pay them anything because their governments are such total puppets in the hands of our government, which is also itself just a puppet in the hands of fatcat American capitalists, the *assholes* who are really running the world. Then, after saying all that (I didn't say assholes), I pointed to the banana-lady on the label again and said in this real sort of puzzled voice, "So tell me. Why is this woman smiling?" Then I walked over to the waste basket by Dr Zimmerman's desk and dropped the banana and returned to my seat.

Soon as I sat down, though, I started shaking so much my teeth were clicking and I had to leave and get a drink of water and walk around the hall for a minute. Then I came back and I shouldn't say this but I think mine was by far the best presentation.

Anyway, that's the most interesting thing lately, so I'll say goodbye for now. Write to me again.

Sam

Dear Sam,

That was really interesting about the banana.

Want to hear something? Doris came up to me in the hall today and started asking me how I've been and how come I've been ignoring her. Which I could see right away meant she was having second thoughts about needing too much room to breathe. But I just acted real casual because I think you were probably right about depending on people too much because I think maybe I was. Anyway, we talked for a while about our classes and such and I think we'll probably start going out again, from the way she told me she still has the same phone number. I'm not going to call her right away though.

Dad broke his left thumb at work. He's okay.

Bye, Sam.

Len

Dear Len,

Tell Dad I'm sorry about his thumb.

I want to tell you about tonight but first let me say something about your intention to act "casual" with Doris. Len, don't play games with people. The world is already filled to the brim with lies and deception. That's how we ended up in Vietnam. Which is exactly what Dr Zimmerman was saying at this rally I went to tonight.

They've been holding them every Wednesday at the lagoon but I always felt funny about going, not knowing anyone, but then I saw this announcement that said Dr Zimmerman would be one of the speakers this time.

Well, there must have been around 250 people there, so I guess it was pretty stupid to feel funny about attending. Dr Zimmerman was the first one up (they had a platform with a microphone) and I could hardly watch, he looked so nervous in his big long coat and ear muffs and mittens and his glasses with that band-aid I told you about. He tried to raise the microphone, being so tall, but he couldn't get it (nobody came up to help) so he had to stoop way down to speak, and as soon as he did, the mike let out with this long scream and this guy right near me goes "Oh wow!" like he was so-o-o stoned and everybody laughed like that was so humorous and groovy. You should have seen how pleased the guy looked.

Anyway, Dr Z just waited, like I did with my banana presentation when people laughed, and then he began again, a little further from the mike, and he was fine, not as good as he is in class but everyone gave him a real loud ovation when he finished, so I was glad. He kept nodding and holding up his mitten while he got down. I couldn't see where he went.

The rest of the speakers were all just students, and I hate to say this but you could tell they were mostly just interested in being up there. Also, not to brag, but my banana presentation would have been twice as informative and coherent as any of theirs. But now I'm being small.

Anyway, the best part was afterwards when everyone started doing a song together. I guess they do it after every meeting. I'd heard the song before. It goes:

We shall overcome
We shall overcome
We shall overcome someday
Oh deep in my heart I do believe
We shall overcome someday

Right away everyone started holding hands with the person next to them, so I'm thinking "let me out of here," but then here were these two hands, from the guy on my left and the girl on my right, so what could I do? We were all wearing gloves but I still felt pretty damn strange. Plus, everyone started swaying back and forth while they sang, so I had to do that too or look like a crank. I kept waiting for the song to end but everyone just kept singing it over and over, louder and louder. You should have heard how it sounded, Len. Five hundred people, all singing together in the darkness under the cold, cold stars. I ended up singing too, real quiet at first, but then a little louder, and louder, then right out loud along with everyone else, holding hands and swaying back and forth, singing as loud as I could but not even hearing myself because it was all just one big sorrowful voice, the voice of the people, the voice of the oppressed. I was almost crying. In fact I was, a little.

Then the song started petering out and everybody took their hands back and noticed how cold out it was and started heading home in all directions. I stayed for a while, just walking around the lagoon.

Anyway, I might as well tell you: I've decided to join the Movement.

That's all I can say for now.

Peace,

Sam

Sam,

That was a good description of the rally.

I was telling Doris about it today in her car in the school parking lot (her mom's car really) and she got all worked up about her brother being in the Coast Guard risking his life to protect our country and how you and all those other people were traitors. I told her you weren't a traitor and that she didn't even know you and so maybe she should just shut up. So then she said I was a Communist sympathizer and please leave the car. Which I did, gladly.

So that's that, and this time for good.

Dad's thumb is better. He went back to work today.

See you.

Len

Dear Len,

Sorry to hear about you breaking up with Doris again, but let's face it, it's time for people to make up their minds which side they're on and it sounds to me like she's made her decision. I just hope that you've decided too and that you're on the side of universal peace, brotherhood and freedom, because I'll tell you the truth, Len, there's going to be a Revolution. I'm talking about a total, complete overthrow. All the combined forces for a whole new world are going to sweep across this country like a tidal wave and I feel very, very sorry for anyone who happens to be in our way, including my roommate and his oh-so-groovy buddies. They probably think they're part of the Movement because they have long hair and take drugs, but they're not, believe me. The Movement is looking for people willing to make sacrifices, suffer and, yes, even possibly die. I would try to tell them this but what's the use, I know how they think of me. So fuck them.

Anyway, like one of the speakers at this week's rally was saying, it's time for those of us truly in the Movement to begin thinking about our individual roles. I've been thinking very carefully about mine and I've decided: Protest Singer/Songwriter. I think that's where I could possibly help the most. The thing is, you don't have to be all that good an actual singer. In fact it's better if you're not, because that will show you're truly sincere and not just some singer. There's this guy Bob Dylan they play on the school station a lot and you should hear *his* voice. He relies almost totally on sincerity.

Except he also plays guitar, which probably isn't that hard to learn once you *have* a guitar. And call it luck or fate but there's a guy on the floor trying to sell a steel string Gibson acoustic, which is what protest singers mostly use, shoulder strap and carrying case included, $75, an unbelievable deal. Trouble is, all I've got is $27. I don't know where the rest of it went except I've been eating out a lot instead of at the dorm which is a difficult place to swallow your food with so many laughing assholes around. I would hit up Dad but he just sent me some money last month. Hell, I even thought of asking *you* for it, as a short-term loan of course, since I know you've got at least fifty saved from your window-washing, just sitting there in your drawer. But I really can't see asking you for that kind of money, even though you'd have it back in no time, so forget I even brought it up. Funny though, I keep thinking how everyone has a part in the Movement and this could be your part for now. But like I said, let's just drop it. I guess what bothers me most, though, is the thought of this beautiful instrument being sold to someone with probably no interest in using it to help the Movement but just wanting to be another hot dog with a guitar. Oh, well.

Anyway, listen, tell Dad I'm real glad to hear his thumb is doing better. And you take care of yourself, little buddy, okay? Meanwhile, here's a little something from Dylan:

> *The old road is rapidly fading –*
> *Please get out of the new one if you can't*
> *lend a hand!*

Peace, love and brotherhood,

Sam

Dear Sam,

All right, here's the money but I'm not doing it for the Movement and I want it back. And I didn't have fifty, I had thirty-eight, the other twelve is from Doris. I lied about what it was for, since you're a Communist to her and should be in prison or shot. I don't agree but I want every penny back, Sam, by July first.

Anyway, we're back together again. I took her over to Eddie's tonight. It was her idea. She wanted to meet him. It went really bad. But then afterwards she had her mom's car and we drove to Carver Park and I feel a little funny telling you this but we ended up having sex together. I shouldn't even talk about it but I had to tell somebody. It was really something, Sam. That's all I'm going to say because I shouldn't even be talking about it.

Well, enjoy your guitar and you can stop calling me little buddy now and here's a little something from me —

> *Pay me back by the first of July*
> *Or else my friend you will surely die.*

Len

13

SUNDAY AFTERNOON

1.

Sam stood outside the open bathroom door, adjusting the shoulder strap of his guitar. There was no one else home — his folks were at Len's Connie Mack League playoff game. In the bathroom, over thirty-five hundred people sat waiting for him.

He strummed a C chord, string by string, to check the tuning one more time. The B string still seemed a little bit flat, and he worked on it.

They were growing impatient in there. A few had begun clapping and stamping. Others joined in. Soon, the whole auditorium was clapping and stamping as one. Then a chant went up:

We-want-Sam! We-want-Sam! We-want-Sam!

It was time. He drew a long breath, let it out, and entered the bathroom.

The place went up for grabs.

He stood in front of the mirror over the sink, nodding sadly, waiting for them to settle down. At last he spoke, quietly, into the microphone:

"Thank you."

They were silent.

"I'd like to begin with something I wrote this morning in my hotel room," he said. "It's a song about — well, about what's going on. About the chaos. About the hate. About the sorrow." He lifted his voice: "And about the murder of men, women and children in the villages of Vietnam!"

He let them go wild, stepping over to the toilet to pee.

Returning, he silenced them with a loud sudden C chord. And for a while he just stood there strumming — C and F, C and F — with his head tilted in a sad question. Then he closed his eyes and in a harsh, taut, nasal voice began to sing:

> *Oh, how many layers of total hypocrisy*
> *Before we can finally begin to take stock and see*
> *That making the world safe for democracy*
> *Is just an excuse for our imperialistic policy . . .*

Now and then as he sang through the several verses he opened his eyes to observe for a while the thin, sad, earnest figure before him.

> *. . . The question, my friends, is twirlin' in the breeze.*
> *Yes, the question is twirlin' in the breeze.*

He finished with an ominous A minor chord instead of C, and stood there, his face full of woe as he listened with them to the dark chord fading away.

Then the dam burst.

"Thank you!" he cried against the roar. "Thank you very much! You're very kind! Thank you! That's enough now! Thank you! For my next number —"

But they only grew louder and wilder.

"People, please!" he shouted, holding up his hand and shaking his head. This wasn't what he wanted. He was no messiah. "Please!" he cried out. "I'm just a singer of songs! I'm just a voice! Crying in the wilderness!"

It was no use — because it wasn't just his music or its message but *him* they wanted, him they craved.

"People, please," he repeated weakly.

Then one of them, a willowy, milk-skinned, raven-haired woman in a long black dress, stepped into the aisle, and everyone else died away.

She approached, very slowly, staring straight in his eyes, and stood before him . . .

Then he saw himself, standing there, still holding up his hand.

He sighed, and left the bathroom.

Back in his room he locked the door, flopped onto his bed and began unbuckling his pants.

He hated Sunday afternoons.

2.

What an ending to my Connie Mack League career.

A playoff game against Hadley Glass for the pennant, with my parents *and* Doris in the stands, and sure enough, it comes down to the bottom of the last inning, game tied 3-3, and guess who's at the plate leading off.

Well, I came through. I got a walk, went to second on a roller to short, made it to third on a long fly to right. And then, with two outs now, I raced for the plate on a passed ball and dove headfirst under the pitcher's tag, the umpire going, "No, he's there! He's safe!"

A great moment.

Except, before I could even get up, Brian Gallagher, who'd been batting, jumps on my back, shouting "We're number one! We're number one!" Then Krueger from the on-deck circle jumps on *him*, and then everyone from the dugout arrives, piling on, and I panicked, I started kicking and working my elbows and got somebody good, Gallagher I guess, and he starts flailing away and gets somebody else, who goes ape, and pretty soon the whole pile is kicking and punching and gouging and swearing, and I could hear Mr Disalvo shouting "*Stop it! Stop it!*" But it was a long time before we finally did.

Then everybody just real quietly got their stuff from the dugout and left, like we'd lost.

On the drive home my mom kept staring out her window not saying anything, looking pretty shook. My dad at least remembered how it all started, mentioning what a nice slide I made. Doris kept fussing over my fat lip, overdoing it for my parents.

Later in my room, taking off my uniform for the last time, I felt sad about such an ugly ending. Sam was there, on his bed with his guitar and his ash tray, and I told him about the game and about the fight afterwards.

He thought it was hilarious. He thought it was the funniest thing he'd ever heard. He sat there rocking and laughing, and I said to him, "So how was *your* afternoon?"

That shut him up.

14
SAMLET

With an hour to kill before his next class, Sam was entering the student union for some coffee and to write a birthday letter to Len, when he noticed a bulletin taped to the glass door:

Auditions for Shakespeare's Hamlet will be held in the University Theater, Wed., Oct. 23, 8 p.m. Please come prepared to perform a 3-5-minute piece of your choice.

Oct. 19

Dear Len,

Happy birthday! How you been? Get this, I've decided to be an actor. They're doing Hamlet here, the greatest play ever written, and I've got a damn good shot at the lead. I know exactly how I'll play it: Hamlet as a man suffering from a state of acute philosophical paralysis, summed up in one line — "To be or not to be" — which I'll deliver with an ironic smile and a sigh of disgust and a cold hopeless pain in my eyes. Wonder what my costume will be like. No leotards please. They should do it in modern dress to show the timelessness. Hamlet in jeans and a Grateful Dead t-shirt. Maybe I'll mention it to the director.

Anyway, how you been? Good, I hope.

Well, I'd better go. Got some lines to memorize. Have a good birthday!

Samlet

"First of all, I want to thank you for coming tonight. I see some familiar faces, and also many new ones. That's good. My name is Dr Abernathy, please call me Frank. Now, we have a goodly number of people here and not a great deal of time. So, what I want from tonight is a look at you: how you move, how you speak, how you be*have* up here. I'll call your name, you'll come up and present your piece, and you'll be free to leave. Tomorrow morning I'll be posting a callback list in the lobby. Those will be the people I think should continue coming. If your name is not on the list, please realize it's because I felt there wasn't a part for for you in *this* production, that's all. So, let's get started." He consulted the sheaf of papers in his hand. "Robert Sorenson?" he said, and looked around.

"Here I am." Someone tall and scrawny stood up near the front, hurried sideways into the aisle and trotted up to the stage, while Dr Abernathy took a seat in the front row. "The speech I'm about to perform for you tonight," Sorenson announced, loud and clear, "is taken from that marvelous work by Tennessee Williams, *The Glass Menagerie*, act four, scene five, spoken by the character Tom." He turned his back to the audience for a moment. When he turned around again he was wearing a sad-and-weary face. "'I didn't go to the moon,'" he said quietly, looking off. "'I went much further. For time is the longest distance between two places . . . . '"

Fake, thought Sam from his aisle seat in the last row.

Sickening. Get off the stage, faggot. Booo . . . Booo . . .

"Fine," said the director when Sorenson had finally finished, "thank you. All right, how about . . . Mary Callahan?"

"Yes," a small voice answered across the aisle from Sam, and a small, pretty, sad-looking girl he hadn't even noticed stood up and hurried nervously down to the stage.

The fair Ophelia, he thought, and sat up straight.

"This is from *Much Ado About Nothing* by William Shakespeare," she said quietly, and stood there looking straight ahead, arms at her sides, like someone about to do a difficult dive off the high board. Then she struck her hands to her hips, tossed back her head, delivered a loud empty laugh, and with the semblance of a British accent shouted, "'By my troth, I have no moral meaning! I meant plain holy-thistle! You may think, perchance, that I think you are in love! Nay . . . '"

Sam couldn't watch. He carefully pulled out a folded notebook from his coat on the seat beside him and began going over once again the stage directions he'd written for himself . . . . "Fine," he heard Dr Abernathy tell her. "Thank you."

Sam watched her come quickly down the little steps and up the aisle. As she passed him, grabbing her coat on the fly, he nodded and held up his thumb, but she didn't see.

"Allen Bergstein?"

"*Steen*, Frank."

"Sorry."

Sam returned to his notebook: To be *(looking off with pain and slight ironic smile)* or not to be. That *(pause)* is the question. *(Move slowly to right, holding up philosophical finger)* Whether 'tis nobler in the mind *(touch left temple)* to suffer the slings and arrows *(hands up against slings and arrows)* of outraaaageous fortune, or to take arms *(motion of unsheathing a sword)* against a seeeea of troubles and by opposing *(thrust with sword, then pause, looking down at victim)* end them. *(Back away from victim, thinking of death, turn to audience)* To die *(pause, 2, 3)* to sleep *(close eyes, speak dreamily)* and by a sleep to say we end the heartache *(open eyes, full of profound heartache)* and the thousand natural shocks . . .

"Sam Rossini?"

He sat there.

"Sam? Rossini?"

People were looking around. Sam looked around, too.

"Okay," the director said, "how about . . . "

"Here!" blurted Sam, and stood up.

"Here who?"

"Rossini."

"*Well.* Sorry to wake you," said the director, and got a laugh.

Sam walked towards the stage, eyes lowered, his breath coming shallow and icy. And with nowhere else to hide he crawled down deep inside of Hamlet, prince of Denmark, prince of pain, letting *him* be out there instead.

He slowly mounted the steps, the cold stone steps of Elsinore Castle, walked heavily to center stage, and did not introduce his speech, because he was thinking, pondering, and he said it out loud: "'To be, or not to be.'"

That was the cold question he had, which led to other questions, and he laid them out as they came to him, words following thoughts, gesture and expression coming too, unbidden, nothing from his notes, and he was already halfway through the speech before a small voice in the corner of his mind observed how good he was doing, how *absorbed* he was, and to drown out the voice he spread his arms and shouted the line, "'For who would bear the whips and . . . and . . . whips and . . . '"

He stood there with his arms out.

"For who would bear all this?" he muttered, to finish, and was about to step down but someone snickered, and he stayed where he was.

He raised a philosophical finger. "For what is Man?" he asked, and crossed slowly to his left. "What is Man but a . . . but a pompous . . . pitiful . . . petrified player upon a stage?" He faced front and held out his empty hands: "Without a script, without a . . . cue, making a frantic . . . fraudulent . . . farcical . . . fool of himself. Ah, verily!" he shouted towards the balcony, spreading his arms once again. "Tis so! Tis so!" He held the pose a moment, then dropped his arms and looked with weariness and some contempt at the faces, before adding quietly, "Tis truly so." Then he walked, wearily but in wild secret triumph, down from the stage. "Fine," said the director, "thank you. Okay, let's see . . . Michael Potter?"

"Right here, Frank."

There was a letter in his box the next morning, from Len. He left the lobby with it, a good hour before his ten o'clock political science class, and read it on his way to the theater.

Dear Sam,

That's really great about being in the play. You're in it but you don't know which part you're playing yet, right? That's what I told Mom and Dad. Mom said for me to tell you to break a leg, which means good luck. Never heard that one before. Dad was saying you would probably be really good because of how good you are at telling lies. He wasn't cutting you down, he was just saying.

So when is it? Doris says we should all read the play first and then it would be more interesting, to see how you do. Will that make you nervous, us being there? If it does, that's show biz!

I had a real good birthday. Finally got hockey gloves. Doris gave me a tie with my initials. Eddie gave me a goldfish.

Well Sam, or should I say Samlet, break some legs!

Len

He put the letter in his pocket and continued walking towards the theater, picturing the four of them sitting out there opening night, close enough for him to see them, see them watching him — watching *him*, Sam, not Hamlet. He'd be going on about the slings and arrows, and there they'd be: Len with a goofy, embarrassed grin . . . his mother looking worried about him playing such a depressed person . . . his father wondering what next, ballet? . . . Doris checking the text to see if he skipped anything . . . .

He entered the lobby. There was no one around. A sheet of paper was taped to one of the auditorium doors and he walked over to it.

Callbacks for Hamlet

He looked down the list of names. He looked down the list again. He turned and walked out of the building.

Heading for the student center, coffee and a cigarette, he despised himself for feeling relieved.

Dear Len,

Just wanted to say I'm glad to hear your birthday was a good one. Hockey gloves at last. I'm sure they'll improve your performance. Speaking of performances, I decided to drop out of that play I mentioned. Had some basic disagreements with the director. I finally said to him, "Look, you want to turn this into a Broadway show? Fine. Have a ball. I'm out of here." I was pretty angry. I still am. Anyway, bye.

Sam

15
LEN, HEATHCLIFF, AND DORIS

I was late. I was supposed to be there before eight so we could watch this movie she wanted to see, called *Wuthering Heights*. Get this. She'd already seen the thing twice, and then she read the book in her English class, and now she wanted to watch it again. I'm talking about Doris. She was baby-sitting at the Millers', over on Cherry. We were going to watch her movie, eat some popcorn, make out a little on the couch during commercials. That was the idea.

The reason I was late, I'd been over at Eddie's house watching the Blackhawks-Bruins game. I told him I could only stay for the first period, but it turned out to be a very long one, a couple of fights, a lot of penalties, and I couldn't leave because Eddie gets kind of upset. Hurt.

But so does Doris.

So anyway I get there and she's mostly just mad, especially when I tell her where I was. She's against me hanging around with Eddie because of him being retarded. And she says I've spoiled the point of the whole evening because the movie's practically half over now and there's no use watching the rest of it and she turns it off and sits on the couch and starts flipping through a magazine.

I tell her to turn it back on. I tell her I know the story,

you've told it to me a hundred times.

Well, she's very sorry she's such a bore.

I decided to take charge. I turned the TV back on and came over to the couch and sat beside her. "Who's that?" I said, "Heathwood?"

She gives this gigantic sigh. "Heath*cliff*," she says. "And no, that's Hindley, and I don't want to *watch* it," and she gets up and goes over to it again. "Here," she says and finds the Black Hawks game and comes back to the couch and her magazine, sitting about a hundred yards away from me.

I say to her, "Dee, come on, you don't want to watch this."

She doesn't answer.

I wasn't sure what to do, so I just kind of watched the game. It was pretty early in the second period, still 2-1, Bruins, both teams with a man in the penalty box. Then Hull takes the puck from behind his own net, charges all the way up the ice, crosses the blue line, winds up and lets go with a fifty-foot slap shot into the upper corner of the net. I go, "Yes! God, do you be*lieve* that guy?"

She looks at me. "I don't believe *you*," she says, and gets up and goes into the kitchen.

I waited real quick for the replay, and went out there.

She was standing with her back against the sink and her arms folded, crying a little. Sometimes when she gets mad she starts crying instead of fighting. She always goes somewhere else to do it, though. Which always leaves me feeling like the heavy. Which I guess in this case I really was, because right on the counter top was a package of Jiffy Pop, with a big empty bowl right next to it, all set. She had this nice idea, the movie and some popcorn, and I'd ruined it.

I came up and put my arms around her. I told her I was sorry.

She put her arms around me and we stood there like that. I told her I wanted to watch the movie. She shook her head, no. I told her I really did. I said I'd heard so much about everybody in it, I wanted to see what they looked like, especially Heathcliff, since he sounded like the guy she liked best.

She mumbled something against my collar.

I said, "What?"

She said, "He looks like you."

I said, "Really?" She was coming around.

"A little taller," she said.

She probably meant a lot taller but I didn't mind. I said, "Let's go watch the rest of it. Come on. Okay?"

She nodded her head. "Let me just check on him," she said, meaning the baby. She went into his room, off the kitchen. She's a very good baby-sitter.

I went back to the TV and kept my hand on the knob and when I heard her coming I flipped it back to the movie. "Now, who's that?" I said, heading back to the couch. "Is that Heathcliff?"

She laughed. "That's Joseph, the servant."

I sat and put my arm around her and she snuggled up. We were back. I was glad. I gave her a kiss on the temple. She didn't turn so I put my fingers under her chin to tilt her face up to mine but she wouldn't.

"Watch," she said, "okay?"

I watched. It's a very old movie, black and white, and it all takes place around a hundred years ago and all the actors are English and speak in a very sophisticated manner, and it was extremely boring.

I was kind of interested in seeing Heathcliff, though, since I was supposed to look like him, only shorter. But he wasn't around at that point in the story. And then a commercial came on, with this little hand puppet for Kraml milk, and I said, "Is *that* Heathcliff?" Which cracked me up. I have this bad habit of laughing at my own jokes.

Doris wasn't laughing at all, though. She was just looking at me. And the trouble was, I couldn't stop laughing. You know how you get sometimes. I kept saying, "I'm sorry," and shaking my head and trying to stop, but I couldn't, and by the time I finally pulled myself together she was sitting up straight with her arms folded, staring at the screen, even though it was still just commercials.

"Dee."

"What."

"Don't be mad. Come on." I put my arm around her again but she stayed the way she was. "I was just making a little joke. That's all I was doing."

She goes, "Shh."

The movie was back on.

Now that's something I really, really hate. When somebody goes "Shh" like that. I mean, that's something you'd say to a little kid. I took my arm back.

I don't think she even noticed, though. Too interested in her boring movie. I just sat there. I was thinking I should have left the Blackhawks game on. I mean, if we're going to be mad at each other *any*way.

Then a butler came into the room — in the movie — and said there's a Mr Heathcliff at the door. I'll admit I was interested. I waited. Then he walked in.

All I can say is, I was very disappointed. I didn't like his looks at all. He was dressed okay but he looked like some kind of *Turk* or something. I don't think I look *that* Italian. I think I'm a pretty regular-looking guy, you know? This guy looked like a tango dancer or something. I didn't make any comments, though. I was still being mad about that "Shh".

But get this. All of a sudden Doris has her head against my shoulder again. And not only that, she's also got her fingers at the back of my neck, touching me in a very sexy manner. Which is something I should mention about her. She can be very, very sexy.

Well, I decided to forget about being mad at her. I put my arm around her shoulder again and closed my eyes. Then I couldn't stand it anymore and went after her.

She gave me this pop-eyed look like I fell through the ceiling, and yelled, "Stop!" And I don't think she meant to but she lifted her knee right straight into my groin.

I rolled off onto the floor, onto my hands and knees, and started taking long deep breaths. I've been hit there before, in hockey, so I know the procedure. Even so, I thought I was going to black out.

Doris was right away down there with me, though. She kept stroking my hair and calling me "honey" and saying she didn't mean to and how sorry she was.

One thing about being hit in the groin, it goes away after only a couple of minutes, so pretty soon I was okay. But I liked the way she was carrying on, and I laid down flat and kept breathing like I was still in pain, and she got down closer, and I turned real slow, like I was still very woozy, and put my arms around her kind of slowly and pulled her against me and went at her neck. But right away she started patting my back, which is what she does when she means this is nice, this is an affectionate hug, and I love you too, and that's enough now, that's enough.

I let go of her. She gave me a kiss on the forehead and said real sweetly, "You okay?"

I nodded but I felt like saying No, I'm not okay and I bet you wouldn't kick *Heathcliff* in the balls if he made a pass at you. I was starting to understand, you see, what all that touching the back of my neck was about.

She got up and held out her hands to help me stand. I said, "I'm all right," and got up by myself. I was feeling cranky.

We went back to the couch. She let me sit first, still being a nurse. Then she sat real close and kind of played with my hair and asked me how I felt. The thing is, there were commmercials on, you see. But as soon as the movie was back, forget it, I wasn't even there.

Just to see, I said to her, "Boy, I'm feeling kind of... I don't know ... kind of *light*-headed."

She patted my leg.

I said, "You know what I think might help?"

She said, "Mm."

I said, "A little popcorn." Actually, I don't even like popcorn. I always get a little piece of it right in the middle of my throat. "I think that would help the wooziness," I said.

She agreed. "There's a package out on the counter top. It's real easy."

I said, "Thanks."

She patted my leg.

I just sat there with my arms folded in a very sulky way, I admit, and watched her damn movie. Which went on and on.

And you know what really struck me? I don't want to go into the details, which would be very boring, but this Heathcliff, that Doris was so in love with, was a total jerk. And I'm not just saying that. He truly was. You should see the way he treated people. I hated him. I hated his guts.

Anyway, there was another commercial break and she came out of her trance and asked me how I was feeling.

I said, "Fine," and kept watching the screen with my arms folded. Okay, I was being a baby.

She moved away from my shoulder and said, "Are you mad at me?"

She said it in a way that means trouble if you don't right away convince her that you're not mad at her at all. But all I did was get up and say real cold and polite, "Would you excuse me? I have to use the bathroom." Good thing I'd been there before so I knew where the bathroom was. That would have ruined it if I had to come back and ask. Anyway, I went in there and I did have to pee, so I took care of that, but then I didn't feel like going back until I was sure the movie was on again, not wanting to fight.

I didn't know what to do with myself while I waited, so I ended up kind of looking in the mirror. I tried to see how she saw me as looking like Heathcliff, only shorter and — I figured — twerpier. I hate to even admit this but I tried giving my hair a little twirl in the front, the way his was. I even tried out something I could say when I went back. I said, real quiet, "Doris, you are mine. A thousand Heathcliffs cannot stand between you and I." Then all of a sudden I thought, What are you *doing*? And got out of there.

Just as I got back a voice was saying, "We now return for the conclusion of *Wuthering Heights*." So that was good. I sat down next to her, but without either of us touching.

She must have told me the story a hundred times, so I knew the ending. Catherine dies and Heathcliff goes on living for a while and then he dies while chasing her spirit around the moors in a blizzard, and they finally get together as ghosts.

So here was this scene now with Catherine dying in her bed and Heathcliff comes in and she opens her eyes and she's always loved him even though she married this other guy Edgar. Or Hindley. I can't remember. One's her brother. Anyway, all of a sudden, guess what. Doris has her head on my shoulder again. Except this time I didn't put my arm around her because it's not even me, you see? It's the movie. So I'm sitting there, not putting my arm around her shoulder, and pretty soon I hear this sniffling. But I still don't even care, because if I wasn't there she'd be sniffling against the back of the couch or something, you know?

But then Catherine wants Heathcliff to help her over to the window so they can look out at the moors where they used to frolic around together, and now Doris is starting to really seriously cry, with her shoulders going and everything. So I put my arm around her. "Hey," I said.

Well, she got a little better. But then Catherine all of a sudden went dead, right there at the window, and Heathcliff lifted her and carried her back to the bed, and Doris started up again.

I kept patting her shoulder and saying, "It's okay, it's okay." She settled down a little when Catherine's husband came in with the doctor, but then while they were all praying over her body Heathcliff launches into this big wild prayer of his own, about wanting her ghost to haunt him for the rest of his life, and Doris went off again, only worse than before. She was almost practically sobbing now, and I said, "Dee. Hey. Come on, you know? It's just a movie."

"Will you please," she says in this loud choking voice, "be *quiet*?"

I thought I was trying to be nice. Wrong again.

I said, "Sorry. Thought it was just a movie. I didn't know this was real." I couldn't stop. "I thought they were just actors. Please forgive me." She got up and went over and turned the channel to the hockey game. "*Okay?*" Her face was all smeared. "*Okay?*" She went into the kitchen.

So there I was, the heavy again.

It looked like the Hawks had a power play going, passing back and forth inside the blue line, but I turned it off and went into the kitchen.

She was standing exactly like before, with her arms folded and her back against the sink, but when she saw me she turned around.

I came up behind and put my arms around her, real carefully, and spoke at her ear. I said, "Dee."

No response.

I said, "Dee, you were crying. What was I supposed to do?" — even though I knew I was supposed to *let* her cry because she enjoyed it: Heathcliff and Catherine and the moors and the tragicness of life, and I was just a short little guy who only cared about hockey and sex and popcorn. Which isn't true.

She just kept staring out the window over the sink.

I felt like bringing things to a head. I said in her ear, like a secret, "Only a movie, Dee."

She turned around and shoved me. She can get wild. "Leave me alone!" she said, crying. "Go watch your hockey game! Go back to Eddie's! You're both about the same speed!"

That was a really nasty thing to say.

I said, "I'm going. But you know what?" I stepped closer. I didn't really know what I was going to say.

She said, "What." She looked nervous, like maybe I could rear back and smack her.

I said, "Say goodbye to your boyfriend for me, even though he doesn't exist. Even though he's just a . . . just a guy in a *movie*."

She nodded her head. "You're just jealous because he happens to be about fifty times more romantic than you'll *ever* be."

"And taller," I said. "Don't forget taller." I started to leave. She goes, "Oh, don't be so pitiful."

I turned back. "*Me*?" I said. "*You're* the one who's in love with some guy in a movie. And you know what else? You know how *old* that guy is by now? Probably about eighty. He probably can't even use the bathroom by himself. He probably has to have somebody—" I stopped. The baby was crying, or I should say screaming.

Doris gave me this "nice going" look and went to his room.

I didn't know what to do. This was one of the worst fights we'd ever had. I felt like I should just leave, especially after that crack about Eddie. That just seemed totally low and uncalled for. But all I did was kind of wander back into the living room. I felt all torn open.

I turned on the TV. The Hawks' Keith Magnuson and the Bruins' Bobby Orr were going at it, gloves off. Magnuson's jersey was pulled up so you could see all his pads and stuff. Right now they were just holding on to each other's shoulders, waltzing around. Then all of a sudden Magnuson started slamming his fist against the side of Orr's head – *bam! bam! bam!* – and the crowd got loud and the announcer started shouting and *I* was shouting, going "Yes! Yes! Yes!"

Then, don't ask me how I knew, but I turned around and there was Doris, standing by the couch with the baby, both of them looking at me.

I turned the TV off. "That Magnuson," I said, jerking my thumb at the TV, shaking my head, "he's a . . . he's really. . ."

She said, "I want to apologize for what I said about Eddie. I shouldn't have said that." She said it real flat, like she was reading it. Then she turned around and walked back.

I stuck my hands in my pockets and followed her, back to the baby's room. I stood in the doorway. It was dark but you could see from the kitchen light. She was setting him down very carefully into his crib. But as soon as he knew what was happening he started crying again. "All right," she said and lifted him out, and he stopped, like one of those dolls. She walked him back and forth beside the crib.

I tried to think of something to say, to be a part of this. "What about his mouthpiece?" I asked.

"It's called a pacifier."

"Right."

"I tried that," she said, walking him, patting his back. "He's just upset."

"From us," I said.

She nodded.

"Tell him I'm sorry," I said.

She said to him, "We're sorry."

That's how she put it: *We're* sorry.

I watched her walking back and forth with him. And I started thinking, Wouldn't it be great? Wouldn't it be great if this was our kid and this was our house and I was the husband and she was the wife?

I said, "Dee?" — a little loud.

She said, "Shhh."

It didn't bother me this time. She set him into his crib again, like he was made of glass, and waited over him. He stayed asleep. I stepped backwards into the kitchen, and she came walking out on eggs, and very slowly closed the door.

Then we just kind of stood there. Shy.

She said, "Well."

All I could do was shrug.

She lifted her eyebrows. "Popcorn?" she said.

I said that sounded great — even though, like I mentioned before, I don't really like popcorn.

But I just felt really happy.

I was leaning against the refrigerator, watching her at the stove. Then the Millers came barging in.

16
JOANNE

She wasn't pretty but Sam liked the way she sat at her desk, so straight and lady-like, with her head attentively tilted, hands on her desk one upon the other. And whenever Dr Wilson called on her she spoke quietly and to the point, sometimes simply answering, "I don't know."

It was early spring when he finally decided after class one day to ask her if she'd care to join him for a Coke or something at the student center.

"Excuse me," he said, catching up with her in the hallway. She stopped.

"I'm in your poetry class?" he said, pointing back towards the room.

She nodded.

He hesitated. "*When* did he say the test would be?"

"Friday," she answered, and walked on.

"*This* Friday?" he asked, staying with her.

She looked at him briefly and nodded. "Right."

"Sure hope it's not like the last one," he said.

She gave a little groan, agreeing.

He gave a large laugh. "My sentiments exactly!" he said, and held the door open for her.

"Thank you."

Outside, she said, "Well, I go this way."

He told her, "Me, too."

They walked. It was a warm afternoon, the sun going in and out. Sam was careful to keep pace with her, glancing now and then at her feet — remarkably large ones for a girl. "So," he said, "how do you like the class? In general."

She seemed to consider the question carefully. "I like the poems. Some of them. The ones I understand." She shook her head. "That one today, though . . . "

"The cummings?"

"No, I liked that one. I like cummings."

"I do, too," he said. "In fact, I would say he's one of the greatest lyric poets of the twentieth century, if not *the* greatest."

"That other one, though."

"The Stevens."

"I didn't understand that at all," she said, "even after he talked about it." She laughed: "E*specially* after he talked about it."

"Well," Sam began, "essentially —"

"What bothers me, though, is the way he calls on people at random. I hate having to speak in class."

"God," he said, "I know what you mean."

"But you speak up a lot — even without him calling on you."

He wasn't sure whether to feel flattered or embarrassed. "I kind of force myself," he said. "I hate it, though," he added. "And you're right. Calling on people at random. I think it's cruel."

"Well . . . it's not actually *cruel*," she said.

"No, you're right, not actually *cruel*. I didn't mean cruel. I just meant . . . well . . . what you were saying."

"Oh, look."

A small gray squirrel was crawling around by a tree near the sidewalk.

"He must be almost still a baby," she said, crouching as she stepped onto the grass, out of people's way.

The squirrel stopped dead on all fours and looked at her.

"Hi there," she said.

Sam crouched beside her. "Hey, little fella, how you doing?"

The squirrel looked at Sam. Then, as if reaching a decision about him, it raced up the tree and out of sight.

"Aww," she said.

"Actually, they often carry rabies," Sam pointed out. "I mean, technically they're part of the rat family."

"Cute, though, wasn't he?"

"He was. He really was."

They walked.

"So," he said, as casually as he could, "you through for the day?"

"Finally, yes."

"Me too," he said, though he had a sociology class right now.

Up ahead, the sidewalk forked towards the dormitories and towards the student center.

He told himself, Say these words: *Care-for-a-Coke-or-something-at-the-center?*

The four o'clock chimes began from Graham Hall.

She suddenly stumbled, almost falling, and dropped one of her books.

"You okay?"

"Yes, I'm fine."

Someone walking the other way picked up her book. Sam took it. "Thanks," he said, in charge. "Here you go."

"Thank you," she said stiffly.

They walked on.

"I have very big feet," she said, "as I'm sure you've noticed."

"Well ... I have a very big nose," he said, "as I'm sure you've noticed."

She smiled at him. "You don't *trip* over it, though. Do you?"

"Not as long as I keep my head up."

She laughed, and continued looking at him. "You're nice," she said.

He shrugged and looked off, glowing.

They walked along.

She said, "This doctor at my high school told me there was no reason I should trip over my feet any more than the next person. He said it's only when I *deny* the size of my feet. Like when I'm ... *with* someone or ... whatever."

He nodded. They were coming to the fork in the sidewalk. "Care-for-a-Coke-or-something-at-the-center?" he said.

"Sure."

They sat talking across a little table for almost two hours. She was majoring in education and wanted to teach elementary school, had a one-eyed dog back home named Basil and an older, married sister named Alice. Her roommate was kind of moody but they generally got along. Last summer she worked in a Baskin-Robbins and hadn't eaten ice cream since. Her parents were divorced. She liked taking pictures, black and white. She was against the war. She tried mescaline once and got very scared. No mention of a boyfriend.

Sam told her a lot about himself, much of it true.

Afterwards they walked to her dorm, without a stumble. And with very little fuss he asked her out for the following evening, eight o'clock, meet her here. "Just walk around," he said.

"That would be nice."

"Good. Well . . . g'night."

"'night."

She went in.

He walked away, slowly. He wasn't sure but it looked as if he might have a goddam girl friend. And he liked her. A lot. He slugged his open hand and walked along holding his fist.

He wore his best sweater, and when she walked into the lobby she was wearing what looked like maybe *her* best sweater and a little bit of make-up and smiling a big smile. And when she came up to him, saying "Hi," she smelled like heaven.

It was a warm evening for early spring, they agreed, shy all over again as they walked towards the north end of campus, working hard at conversation. But when they reached the lagoon, with its willow trees, and the ducks, and the moon along the water, they both stopped trying so hard.

They sat beneath a tree, her suggestion.

She began telling him about the lagoon concert she'd been to last weekend: Gordon Lightfoot, the whole stage right over there, with a guy on bass guitar and a guy on a little electric piano, and Gordon — she called him Gordon — singing and playing guitar. "God, was he good," she said.

Sam nodded, smoking.

He had made up his mind last night that they were going to be a couple: Sam and Joanne. And he'd also made up his mind that beginning tonight he was not going to say or do a single thing designed to impress her, because she had to like him — possibly love him — exactly as he was, or there wasn't any point to being Sam and Joanne. And so far tonight he had kept his promise. But when she kept going on about "Gordon," he couldn't help inserting that he himself played guitar and in fact had written some fairly decent songs of his own.

She was interested. She asked him what kind of songs he wrote.

"Well," he said, "the music is mostly just variations on your basic three-chord folk melody, but the lyrics are sort of, oh, expressions of Man's essential alienation, I guess you could say."

She nodded carefully. "Is that how you feel, Sam? Alienated?"

He loved whenever she said his name.

"Well, I don't mean just me," he explained. "I'm talking about the human condition. See, that's one of the big differences between Lightfoot's stuff and mine. He's more into just his *own* little feelings, know what I mean?"

"I'd like to hear you play some time."

"Oh, I don't know."

"I really would."

He shook his head, yanking up some grass, and waited for her to urge him one more time.

But she didn't. She looked out at the water. "I saw someone fishing here the other day." She shook her head. "I can't imagine what kind of —"

"I could bring the guitar tomorrow night," he said, "if you'd like."

She turned to him, smiling. "That would be nice, Sam. That would be really nice."

He shrugged, hiding his delight.

They watched the moonlight wiggling along the water. "Someone fishing here, huh?"

That night in his room before going to bed he rehearsed all nine of his songs until his roommate asked him to stop. Please.

The following evening he sat with his back against the same tree, his guitar against his stomach, while Joanne sat on the grass in front of him. Softly strumming, he began quietly singing the first verse of a song he called "The Subject-Object Dualism":

> *The world that is me is all,*
> *The world that is thee is all,*
> *And the distance between us*
> *Is the dark between the stars.*

Strumming through the chords before the next verse, he glanced at her. She was hugging her knees, staring at the grass, listening hard.

Ah shit, he thought. He had promised himself he wasn't going to do this, he wasn't going to try to impress her, and now look at him. He stopped playing.

She looked up.

"It goes on," he said, studying the strings. "But I don't know . . . I mean, it's *kind* of sincere, but it's mostly really just someone trying to write a deep, meaningful song and be a deep, meaningful songwriter." He looked at her. "Know what I mean?"

She nodded, studying him. "You're really honest about yourself," she said, and touched his ankle.

He lowered his eyes, shrugged. He felt like confessing every phony thing he'd ever done.

"Play the rest of it," she said.

"Nah. You're right, it stinks."

"I didn't say that. I don't think it stinks at all."

He looked at her. "Guess I'm no Gordon Lightfoot, am I."

"So?"

"Although, I mean, you figure he's got a *bass* player behind him, and a piano, and a —"

"Sam," she laughed, giving his ankle a shake, "play the rest of it. I really *like* it."

"Seriously?"

"Seriously. I wouldn't just say that."

"Well, what would you say if you *didn't* like it? I'm just curious."

"I'd say . . . 'Gee, that was nice. Do you know any Gordon Lightfoot?'"

They laughed.

"All right," he said, and strummed the opening chord.

"Play it again, Sam," she said, and gave a laugh.

He waited.

"Sorry," she said.

He began playing and singing, this time with feeling.

Saying goodnight that evening outside her dorm, away from the doors, Sam placed his hands on her arms and kissed her carefully on the mouth. She kissed him back, more fully, slipping her arms around him. Then they held each other for several moments, during which he knew she could feel his erection. Then they kissed again, briefly, and whispered goodnight.

He carried his guitar back to the lagoon and sat beneath their tree for a while, vaguely strumming, too happy for his room.

They didn't see each other the following night: she had a

child psychology test to study for, along with their poetry exam. After supper Sam came up to his room and flopped on his bed with his Modern American Poetry text. But he found it hard to concentrate. He kept drifting up from the words, savoring the little ache of missing her, savoring too the possibility that she was looking up from *her* book at that very moment with the same little ache.

But there was something else as well. He'd been grimly avoiding the thought all day, but now he finally had to look at it. The way she kissed him last night and held him even closer as the swelling in his pants grew obvious — was it already time they had sex? Chatting last night between songs, she happened to mention that her roommate went home every weekend. Maybe she said it only in passing, but maybe not. Maybe it was a hint for tomorrow night — his cue. And if he didn't follow up on it, would she begin wondering about him?

He looked at the words in his lap.

"Sam?" she said.

"Yeah?"

"Do you sometimes get real quiet like this? Or is something the matter?"

They were walking back from a free movie at the center, a Czech film with subtitles, most of which he hadn't bothered reading.

"I just sometimes get quiet," he said.

"Okay."

When they reached her dorm they stood along the wall, where he quickly lit a cigarette. "Nice night," he remarked, scanning the stars.

She looked up, and agreed.

"Jo?"

She looked at him.

He took a pull on his cigarette, and began. "The other night? You were talking about your roommate?"

She nodded.

"And you happened to mention she goes home every weekend?"

She nodded.

He drove on. "Well, I was wondering, did she go home *this* weekend?" he asked, hoping the answer was no, because he'd never been to bed with a girl and would make a desperate mess of it and she would feel pity and disgust and he would lose her.

"Yes," she answered, looking him shyly in the eye, "she did."

"I see. Well . . . she must be very fond of her family."

"She has a boyfriend there."

"Ah."

"Would you like to stay with me tonight, Sam?"

"Well," he said, nodding at his feet, "that would be . . . that would be fine."

Standing on the rosy throw rug between the beds, hands in his back pockets, Sam looked around at the posters, dried flowers, figurines and stuffed animals, while Joanne, kneeling on her bed, had trouble lighting a fat white candle on the shelf.

"Very nice," he observed.

"Kind of cluttered," she said.

"Possibly," he allowed. "And yet —"

"There," she said, getting the candle lit. She got up from the bed and walked to the door and switched off the overhead. "How's that?" she asked, in a voice as soft as the lighting.

Sam nodded around at the bobbing shadows on the walls. "Very nice," he observed.

They stood there.

"Mind if I smoke?" he asked, reaching into his shirt pocket.

She sighed and folded her arms and looked away. "If you'd like."

He put the cigarettes back. There was nothing else he could do but walk over to her.

She unfolded her arms.

"Hey," she said to him afterwards.

He was lying naked on his back staring up at the shadows moving around on the ceiling.

She laid her head on his chest. "Don't worry about it. Okay?"

He continued staring at the ceiling.

"You just weren't in the right frame of mind," she said, "that's all."

He wanted to leave.

"Or else . . . " she said.

"What."

"Maybe it was me. Maybe I don't . . . "

"No. You do."

They were quiet.

"One more question?"

"What."

"Was this your first time?"

"Yes. Listen, I'm going to go now."

"No, you're not." She tucked her hands under his back.

They lay there.

After a minute he set his hand on her head.

"This is nice," she said. "Just like this."

He closed his eyes as if this was nice, just like this.

In the morning he woke with his arm across her stomach and his cock as big as could be.

He looked at her sleeping face a moment, then gently kissed her forehead. She remained asleep. He ran his hand along the swell of her hip. "Joanne," he whispered.

"Mm."

"Jo."

She opened her eyes.

"Hi," he said.

She smiled. "Hi."

"Sounded like you were having a bad dream," he told her.

"Really? I don't remember . . . " She noticed his condition. "Wow, Sam."

"Jo." They embraced. In a corner of his mind he wondered about his breath but then she locked her mouth on his and he rolled on top of her. . .

"Easy, Sam. Here, let me help." She helped him.

"Oh," he said, in wonder.

"Yes," she said.

"*Oh*," he said.

"Sam," she said. "*Sam.*"

"*What.*"

"No, don't stop."

He continued.

"Yes," she said. "Oh, Sam, yes . . . *yes* . . . "

"Aw, *God*," he said.

Afterwards, as she nestled against him, he lay there amazed and sated and very, very pleased with himself.

"That was really nice, Sam."

"Well . . . thanks." He patted her rear.

And all he needed right now, he thought, was a cigarette, to be absolutely content.

Sam continued seeing Joanne almost every evening and staying with her on weekends.

For her birthday he wrote a long, difficult song about the importance of human intimacy in a godless universe, and made a tape of it on his cassette recorder. "Jo?" the tape began. "This is for you . . . ."

Their favorite place was the same willow tree beside the lagoon, and one afternoon she took pictures of him sitting underneath it: looking off at a cloud, looking up at the branches, looking deeply into the camera . . . .

He often talked about possibly writing a novel over the summer, something along the lines of *Portrait of the Artist as a Young Man* by James Joyce, only not so damn precious. . . .

And he couldn't help noticing himself getting better and better in bed each time, Joanne often remarking what a wonderful lover he was, and he could tell she wasn't just being nice, that in fact he was like some lean, exquisite animal, the way he worked her — slowly, slowly — until she was lost and moaning his name.

He loved when she got like that, moaning "Sam . . . Sam . . . ."

Then one night, lying loosely in each other's arms, Joanne smiled sleepily into his eyes and said, "I love you."

He smiled sleepily back at her.

But then he saw that she was waiting, and he drew her closer, to avoid her eyes, and said, "I love you, too."

They held each other.

She said, "I feel very close to you right now."

He said he felt the same.

She told him how happy she was.

He said he felt the same.

And when she'd finally fallen asleep, he carefully took back his arms, blew out the candle on the shelf, and lay facing the other way, staring hard at the dark.

After that night Sam began noticing certain things about Joanne that bothered him.

Her humming, for example. Whenever they were quiet for a while she'd begin humming, which wouldn't be so bad if she'd at least try humming a particular actual goddam *tune*.

And he found himself wanting to tell her his opinion of that poster on her wall: a white unicorn on a misty cliff and some dipshit message about following your dreams.

But in fact her appreciation of *any* kind of art was at a rather dipshit level: e.e. cummings. Or the great Gordon Lightfoot. Which of course made any admiration she expressed for his *own* poems and songs pretty meaningless.

And he had to face it: she wasn't very pretty, she just wasn't. Nor was her body much to shout about: miniature tits, hips out to here, and Christ almighty the size of those feet. But what bothered him most was hearing her say his name while they were making love — because it wasn't him, it was this poet-philosopher-songwriter-lover he'd created for her with his verses and his talk and his songs and the things he had learned to do in bed to make her moan his name. And he'd begun imagining while making love that she was a stranger, some desperate nymphomaniac he'd met that night in a bar, and that all she wanted was to fuck, it didn't matter who, and that for some weird reason she called *all* her men "Sam," provided they were hot and huge and hard and pumping like mad . . . .

"Stop!" Joanne said one night, and shoved at his shoulders.

"What!" he said, rolling off. "Jesus."

"You were *hurting* me."

"I was?"

"*Yes.*"

"I thought . . . " He was still out of breath. "Actually, I thought we were going pretty good there."

"Not like *that*." She seemed about to cry, and turned her face toward the ceiling.

He'd never seen her cry before. "Hey," he said, trying to stop her, and put his arm across her stomach.

She turned the other way. She was definitely crying now.

"Jo, don't," he said, "okay? Come on. Please?" If she didn't stop he would have to leave because he couldn't stand this. "I'm sorry, okay? Come on."

She sniffed.

"Okay?" he said.

She sniffed again. "Can I ask you something?"

He didn't like the sound of that. "Sure," he said.

She turned and looked at him, hard. "Do you love me, Sam?" she asked.

He held the challenge in her eyes long enough to say, "Hell, yes." Then, as if hurt by such a question, he said, "Jeez," and moved down to lay the side of his face against her stomach.

After a few moments she put her hand on his head. But he could tell by her stomach she was crying again.

They got up late the next morning and spoke rather politely. After they had showered, Sam using the "weekend men's," it was after eleven. He casually suggested brunch (a word he'd never used before in his life) at a bar and grill in town called The Hobbit Hole, and to hell with the cost.

She looked suspicious.

"Something different," he said. "That's all."

They sat in a booth near the bar. Sam suggested a drink or two before they ate, and after they'd proved to the waitress they were both nineteen he ordered a pitcher of beer.

He smoked and talked about quitting cigarettes as soon as the semester ended, while Joanne continued looking suspicious of all this.

When their beer finally came he poured hers, poured his, and drank his off in three long swills.

"Sam?"

"Yo," he said, pouring another glassful.

"Why are you drinking like this?"

"Thirsty," he explained, and took another long drink.

"If there's something you want to tell me, just tell me, okay?"

He took another quick drink. Then, looking into his glass, he told her there *was* something, actually. He said he'd been thinking. He told her he'd been thinking maybe it wouldn't be a bad idea if they didn't see each other for a while, that he'd fallen behind in his classes and maybe they should just, well, cool it for a while.

She asked him, carefully, what he meant by a while.

He shrugged, looking into his glass. "Couple months," he mumbled.

"I didn't hear you, Sam."

"A couple of months," he said.

Neither of them spoke for a moment. Sam continued

studying the lacework of foam down the walls of his glass.

"School's over in a month," she pointed out, quietly.

He was going to start crying if he didn't get this over with. "I'm sorry, Jo," he said, and looked at her.

She nodded, tears appearing, and was about to say something, but got up quickly and walked out.

He sat there. Then he poured her beer back into the pitcher to prove to himself what a cold-blooded sonofabitch he was.

Three weeks went by and he hadn't seen her except in their poetry class, where now he always took the nearest available seat to the door and slipped out quickly at the end of the hour. Sometimes during class he would catch himself watching her but would immediately begin listening to Dr Wilson with redoubled attention. He no longer volunteered any observations, however.

One night after dinner he walked into town and dropped by The Hobbit Hole, just for the hell of it, and sat in the same booth, and drank a beer, reading a book he'd brought. He came again the next night and drank three beers before leaving, and stopped at the lagoon for a while.

The night after that, a Friday, he was standing with his back against the bar, drinking his fifth beer, when she walked in with someone, a tall skinny bearded guy in a blue beret, sloppy sweater and paint-spattered blue jeans.

They took a table in the far corner of the room.

He sipped his beer and watched them.

Pablo Picasso did almost all the talking, while Joanne sat very straight in her lady-like way, hands on the table one upon the other — exactly the way she had so often sat listening to *him*.

A girl came to their table, took their order, and Picasso

picked up where he'd left off. Then, at an apparently dramatic point in the story of his life and work, he reached across and placed his bony fingers on her hands.

Sam stabbed out his cigarette and walked over, weaving just a little.

"Well!" he said in surprise. "Hi there!"

Joanne looked up. "Oh. Hi."

"How you *doing*?" he asked, hands on his hips, nodding at both of them.

"Jason, this is Sam," she said. "Sam's in my poetry class."

That hurt a bit.

Jason said, "Hello," and held out his hand.

Sam shook it, a little surprised at how rough it felt, but gripped it hard and said, "You're an artist, aren't you. Know how I could tell? Three things." He ticked them off on his fingers: "The beard, the sloppy sweater, the painted-up blue jeans, and most of all" — he winked at Joanne — "the beret."

"That's four," Jason pointed out.

"Excuse me," the waitress announced, with their beers.

Sam moved aside. "Here, let me pay," he said, reaching into his back pocket.

"That's all right," Jason told him.

"No, really," said Sam, pretending his wallet was stuck until Jason had his money out. "Okay," he said, "but the next one's on me. Agreed?" he asked, waiting to be invited to sit with them. But Jason only nodded, paying the girl, and Joanne didn't look up from her glass. "Anyway, listen," he said, "great meeting you, Janus."

"Jason."

"Whatever. And I just want to say, in all sincerity, I really and truly like that little hat." He winked at Joanne again and headed back to his stool.

Sliding aboard he grabbed up his beer and finished it off in one long drink. "*Yo,*" he called to the bartender, wagging the empty glass like a bell.

The bartender brought him another draft.

"Slow night," Sam remarked.

"Early."

"That's true. Here you go. Keep the damn difference."

"It's another dime."

"Right. Here you go. Hey, how 'bout those White Sox?"

"What about 'em?"

"Well . . . how they doing? I was wondering."

"I really couldn't say, man."

"Don't follow it?"

"Not really."

"Well, actually, me neither. I *used* to. I used to be really into baseball. Second base, that was my spot — my *home*, know what I mean?"

"Hang on." Someone down the bar wanted change to use the juke box.

Sam lit a cigarette. Then he set it on the ash tray and pretended to yawn and stretch, turning just enough to look toward their table.

They were gone.

"Second base, huh?" the bartender said, returning.

"What?"

"You were saying."

Sam shrugged. "That's all. That's all I was saying."

"Ever play any hockey?"

"No."

"That was *my* game, man. The most exciting sport in the world. Know why?"

"No."

He woke up late the next morning, hungover, and tried to sleep some more. But he couldn't. He kept picturing Joanne and Jason.

He got up and showered and dressed and went for a long walk and returned, still picturing Joanne and Jason.

He sat on the edge of his bed.

After a minute he went to the phone by the door, lit a cigarette and called her.

No answer.

He sat on the edge of the bed again. He finished his cigarette. Then he went to his desk.

Dear Joanne,

When I told you that day in the Hobbit Hole that I needed some time alone to catch up on my school work, I had no idea you would use that as an opportunity to jump into a relationship with someone else. I honestly thought you had more integrity than that. Guess I was wrong.

Now, I didn't want to embarrass you by saying anything in front of your "boyfriend" last night, but let me tell you now: You and I need to have a very serious talk about what exactly is going on here.

He lit another cigarette.

Also, just as an aside, I must say I find your taste in men a bit bewildering, to say the least. I have met some phony, pretentious people in my time, but this Jason fellow wins the cigar. I know exactly how you think of him: Sensitive Artist. But let me tell you, he's an artist all right, a <u>con</u>

artist. And I'll bet anything his paintings are extremely "abstract" (something like the carefully accidental drops of paint all over his blue jeans) to conceal the lamentable fact that he is a no-talent, utterly bogus fraud. Jo, the guy's making a fool out of you – harsh words, I know, but I say them only because I care very much what happens to you and don't want to see you get hurt – because I love you, still, in spite of your unfaithfulness.

Enough said.

Now, I'm sure you and Jason have "plans" for tomorrow, it being Sunday, but I would very much appreciate your calling me tomorrow night around 10. We have much to discuss.

I'll be waiting.

> *Love,*
> *Sam*

He ran the letter to her dorm, where he asked the woman behind the desk in the lobby to please put this in Joanne Maloney's mailbox, and waited to make sure she did.

Sunday night he sat at his desk vaguely strumming his guitar and drinking from a six-pack of malt liquor talls he'd smuggled up. He waited until eleven, then went to the phone.

Her roommate answered.

"Joanne there?" he said.

"May I ask who's calling?"

"Would you put her on, please."

He waited.

"Hello?" Joanne said.

"Hi. It's me. Sam."

"Hi," she said, dead flat.

"Jo?"

"What."

"Ask you something?"

"What."

"Did you get my letter?"

"Yes."

He nodded. "Why didn't you call me? Can I ask you that?" He waited.

"Jo?"

"Sam, can we talk some other time? I'm very tired right now."

"I see."

"Goodnight."

"Can I ask you something?"

She sighed in his ear. "What."

He put his hand against the wall. "Why you so tired?"

"I don't know, Sam. Maybe because it's rather late at night, you know?"

Sarcasm. He pressed against the wall. "How's Jason?"

"I have to go now."

"See him today?"

"Goodbye."

"*Wait*. Jo. You there?"

"Yes," she sighed.

"Listen. I was wondering . . . Jo?"

"I'm here."

"How you doing?"

"Sam . . . "

"All right. Listen, though. Just . . . tell me one thing?"

"What."

"Jason . . . " He pressed against the wall as hard as he could. "Have you had sex with him? Would you tell me that please?"

She hung up.

He slugged the wall, then dialed her back.

It rang on and on.

He was back at his desk, on his last can of beer, writing a complicated apology, when his roommate walked in from the lounge down the hall where a little group of them played cards every Sunday night.

Sam lit a cigarette and watched him carefully folding his sweater, carefully hanging up his shirt . . . .

"Hey. Carl."

"What."

"You're sort of an art major, right? What the hell's it called again?"

"Graphic Design."

"There you go. Listen. You know a guy named Jason something?"

"No. What the hell you doing with beer in here?"

"Never mind the beer. You don't know anybody at all named Jason?"

"No."

Sam watched him putting on his pyjamas. No one in the world, he thought, wears pyjamas to bed except kids, old men, and this wimp.

"Want to know why I keep asking about a guy named Jason?"

"Not really."

"Well, I'll tell you. I'm gonna kick the sonofabitch's ass, that's why."

"Good for you," Carl told him, setting his digital alarm clock.

"I'm gonna find out where he lives. I'm gonna go over there and I'm gonna knock on his door." He knocked on his desk. "He's gonna open the door, and I'm not gonna say a word. All I'm gonna do is start beating the living shit out of him. Without a word."

"That's the spirit," said Carl, climbing under the blanket. He turned to the wall. "Just hit your light before you leave, will you? Without a word."

Sam looked at him lying there. "You don't believe me, do you."

Carl didn't answer.

"You think I'm just a bullshitter, right? Just a big fucking bullshitter. That's all I am, right?"

Carl still didn't answer.

Sam grabbed one of his empties — "*Right?*" — and threw it at him, hitting the bookshelf.

Carl sat up quickly. "You asshole."

Sam stood. "Come on," he urged, and began dancing like a boxer over to the bed. "You woman," he said, bobbing around and rolling his fists. "Hit me. Come on. Get up and hit me."

Carl got up.

"Let's go," said Sam, dancing in front of him. "You woman. You pussy. Hit me. Come on, hit me. *Hit* me."

Carl swung his fist and caught him square on the cheekbone, almost knocking him down.

Sam came dancing back. "Come on."

They fought.

Sam lost, badly.

He woke in his clothes the next morning. His ribs hurt, his lips felt huge, and the whole left side of his face ached. His roommate's bed was made, the digital clock reading 11:18. He closed his eyes. When he opened them again it was after two. He got up, carefully, and went to the little mirror by the door.

"Good," he whispered, nodding at his battered face. He hoped she was satisfied.

When their poetry class began letting out, he was sitting on the bike rack outside the building, hands in his pockets, a cigarette in his mouth.

She came walking out in his favorite sweater, the yellow one, cradling her books, looking so damn nice.

"Jo," he said, holding his pose.

She turned — and brought her hand to her mouth.

"How you doing?" he said. He drew on his cigarette.

"What *hap*pened?" she said, walking over.

He shrugged. "Nothing. Little difference of opinion. How was class?"

"You were in a fight?"

"Something like that."

"With who?"

"Carl." He shook his head at the silliness of it.

"Your roommate?"

He sighed and told the story: "He comes in the room, and I guess . . . well, I guess he could tell I'd been crying. It was after our phone conversation. Anyway, he knew it must be about you, and so he starts going on about women in general, how they're all bitches, heartless, good for one thing only. It bothered me, that kind of talk. I asked him to stop but he wouldn't. I *told* him to stop and he still wouldn't. So . . . I stopped him."

"The side of your face is all —"

"Hey," he laughed, "it's nothing. You should see *him*." He shook his head and gave a whistle, which hurt. "Anyway, listen, we need to talk. How 'bout a Coke or something at the center."

"No, thank you," she said, suddenly formal. "I'm on my way somewhere."

"Oh." He nodded.

"Well . . . 'bye," she said, and walked off.

"Mind if I walk with you?" he asked, walking with her.

She shrugged.

They walked in the direction of town.

"Where we headed?"

"Jason's," she told him.

He nodded, swallowed. "What's he got, an apartment?"

"Yes."

"Excuse me please!" a girl sang behind him on her bicycle, and he made way, Joanne waiting.

"An apartment," he said, walking beside her again. "That's what *I'm* going to get next year. A little studio or something, you know? With a nice big writing desk. For my work." He looked at her. "My poems, my songs, you know?"

She nodded, looking straight ahead.

They walked for a little while without speaking. Then he said carefully, "Listen. About last night, on the phone. I want to apologize. I was out of line and I want to say right now —"

"Just forget it," she said quietly.

They walked in a deeper silence all the way to the lagoon, and crossed the little wooden bridge that spanned the narrow end.

"Jo, look at the squirrel," he said, and stood pointing up at a tree near the sidewalk. "See him up there? On the branch? He's watching us. See him? On the edge of the branch? See him there?"

"I see him, Sam."

"Cute, isn't he?"

"Yes."

"Squirrels," he said, shaking his head in wonder.

They walked.

There were ducks out on the water, but he couldn't think of anything to say about them.

He finally said, "So," shoving his hands in his pockets, making fists, "tell me. This Jason fellow. Is he pretty good?"

She looked at him sharply.

"*Artist*," he explained. "Pretty good artist?"

She sighed. "He's not an artist, Sam, okay?"

He nodded sadly. "Stuff's pretty bad, huh?"

"I *mean*," she said, looking at him, her face pinched with anger, "he has nothing to *do* with art. He does maintenance work in the dorm and he sometimes wears a beret. All right?"

He shrugged. "All right," he said quietly.

They walked on without speaking, past the lagoon and up to the main street of town, where they waited at the curb for the walk sign, Sam quickly lighting another cigarette. They crossed, and continued down a quiet side street.

"Did a little maintenance work myself last summer," he finally said. "Where my old man works. Guess I told you about that."

"Yes."

"I'll be back again this year," he added.

She nodded.

He pulled hard on his cigarette and tossed it off. "And I'll tell you something: I'm looking forward to it. *Len's* going to be with me now, and I know this sounds corny but I'm hoping I can teach him something. Something about . . . well, about the dignity of labor, you know? I mean, all this poetry and stuff is fine, in its place, but there's something about rolling up your sleeves and working with your hands. It's like . . . well, it's like Robert Frost put it, that line where he says —"

"Sam, stop it." She stood there. "Please?" she asked him. "Just . . . please leave me alone?"

"I can't." His eyes were brimming. "I love you," he said.

She turned her head away.

"Honest to God, Jo."

She looked at him. "No, Sam, you don't," she told him. "Honest to God," she added, and walked away.

He stood there.

"A *janitor?*"

She kept walking.

He swiped at his eyes with his sleeve. "The guy's a *janitor?*"

She walked to the end of the block and went left — stumbled, and quickly recovered.

"Jo," he said quietly.

She continued around the corner and was gone.

Back in his room, hunched over his guitar, he tried singing the blues:

My sugar left me, oh yes she left me, for another man.
My sugar left me, I said she left me, for another man.
And now the pain, yes the pain,
Lord it's more, yes it's more than I can stand.

It wasn't working. He strummed harder, sang louder:

My sugar left me! Don't you know she left me! For another man!

Louder:

I said she left me! That's right, she left me! —

He gave up. He quit playing. And for a long while he just sat there.

17
WEEDING

A sign of *what*?" Len asked.

"A si-ne-*cure*," Sam repeated.

"All right, what's a si-ne-*cure*."

"Figure it out."

They were in a large field behind the power house, in gloves and hard hats, bending and swiping with sickles at the waist-high weeds.

"Something that cures your sinuses?"

"Close. It means a job that doesn't have any purpose to it." Sam paused with his sickle. "I think. Or else a job that doesn't involve any work."

"This wouldn't be a sinecure, then," Len pointed out.

"Unless we just sat here all day," Sam said. "Which we could probably do. I don't think they'd really give a shit."

"Dad would, if he came out and saw us."

"True."

They worked for a while without talking. The morning was muggy and gray, with little rolls of thunder now and then.

"God, this is boring," Len remarked. "This has gotta be the most completely, totally boring job I've ever —"

"Stop whining."

"Well, I'm *tired*. You woke me up last night, the way you

came in. Then I couldn't get back to sleep."

"Sorry."

"You walk around like Frankenstein when you're drunk."

"Did I say anything?"

"Something. I think it was a quote."

"Shakespeare?"

"Sounded like it. Where'd you go, Hazy's?"

"Yeah."

"See anybody?"

"Nah."

"So what'd you do, just sit there getting blasted?"

"For a while. Then I started mingling. I ended up talking to this woman, she must've been almost fifty. Very attractive, though. Very well-preserved."

"What'd you talk about?"

"This and that. She told me what an asshole her husband was. I told her I was an ex-priest."

"She buy it?"

"Yeah. I told her I'd lost my faith and now I was just a drunk."

They worked.

"So, did you . . . leave with her?"

"Nah. I probably could've, though. Except she kept calling me 'Father'."

Len chuckled.

"Actually," Sam went on, "we did go out to her car. She wanted me to hear her confession. I told her I was no longer qualified, but she insisted. So we get in the car and —"

"You making this up?"

"Just this part. So we get in the car and right away she —"

"Let's just stick with reality, Sam."

They worked quietly for a while. The sky muttered.

"How's this for real?" Sam said. "If we work here all summer, know how much we'll make?"

"About two thousand each."

"Not *even*."

"So? That's not bad."

"It's all right for *me*," Sam said. "I've got that grant again. But you're gonna have to take out a pretty sizeable loan before school starts, you know that?"

Len didn't answer.

"Actually, though," Sam continued, "if you stick it out all summer you could probably hit up Dad for the rest, as a loan."

"I don't think I'll be going," Len said, working. "I've been meaning to tell you."

Sam stopped. "What're you talking about?"

"Nothing. I just don't want to go there, that's all."

"Why the hell not?"

Len didn't answer.

"Len, I got that a*partment* for us."

"I know, but . . . " He continued working.

"But you don't want to live with me."

"It's not that."

"Well, what *is* it, then? You want to go to Vietnam? Come home in a box, like Fred Fraley? They're still drafting people, you know."

"No, they're not."

"All right, you want to work at jobs like *this* all your life?"

"I'm going to the community college."

"What, Lewis and *Clark*?"

"Right."

Sam stood there. "Why?"

"Well . . . it's a lot cheaper. You were just saying how —"

"Len, I told you, you can take out a loan, or get it from Dad. No big deal."

Len continued working.

Sam watched him. Then he nodded his head. "*I* know what it is," he said. "What's-her-face is going there. Right?"

Len didn't answer.

"That's a very stupid reason, Len."

Len worked on.

"Very stupid," Sam repeated, and began swiping at the tasselled heads of the weeds. "For some little . . . rat-faced . . . "

"Cool it, Sam," Len warned, and stopped working.

They faced each other.

"Go ahead," Sam told him, "cut my fucking head off."

Len sighed and went back to work.

Sam watched him for a while. "I really and truly cannot be*lieve* what a fool you are, Len."

"Believe it."

"For Boris."

"*Dor*is."

The sky rumbled.

"See?" Sam said. "Even *God* doesn't like the bitch."

Len gave a laugh and stopped himself.

"No, but seriously, Len, all kidding aside, we need to talk this over, you know? We really do. What we need to do here, we need to consider all the various —"

"No, we don't, Sam. I already talked it over with Doris and considered all the various variations, okay?"

"With Doris."

"Right," he said, and returned to his weeds.

Sam stood there for a minute. Then he went back to work,

hacking away until he was exhausted. When he'd caught his breath, he said, "Let me ask you something. No, let me *tell* you something. You know what love is? Between a man and a woman? You know what it is?"

"Here we go."

"Love," Sam said carefully, "is a feeling in the nervous system . . . which Nature has biologically programmed humans to experience . . . in order to guarantee the continuation of the species."

"Thank you, Professor."

"Sounds cold, I know, but that's how the truth often is. Anyway, keep it in mind the next time you're with Doris. Just step back a little from all these deep, wonderful feelings you're having over someone . . . like that, and ask yourself: 'Why?' That's all. End of lecture." He went back to work.

Len stopped working. He took off his hard hat and dragged his forearm down his sweaty face. "Okay if I ask *you* something?"

Sam continued working. "Go ahead."

"How come whenever anything good is going on with me, you try to spoil it?"

"Just telling you what I know, Len, that's all."

"Well, maybe I'm not interested."

"Of course you're not. You just want to be in love. 'Oh, Doris.' 'Oh, Leonard.'"

"Fuck you, Sam."

Sam stopped working and stood looking off at the gray, hanging sky.

"I didn't mean that," Len told him.

Sam continued standing there.

Len went on, "It's just . . . you always act like you're the only one who ever thinks about things. Like everybody else just goes along in a trance or something."

Sam stood there, looking off.

"*I* think about stuff, too, Sam. You know?"

"All right," said Sam, turning to him, "let's hear *your* definition, then."

"Of what."

"Love. I gave you mine. Let's hear yours."

"My definition."

"Right."

"Of love."

"That's right."

"Sam, this is kind of stupid."

"No, it's not. You love Doris, right? 'Fuck you, Doris.' You'd never say that to *her*, would you."

"I said I'm sorry."

"And I accept. I'm just saying, she obviously means a lot more to you than *I* do."

"See how you get?"

"Because here you are, right? Ready to dump all our plans. A beautiful apartment. All the . . . all the *times* we could have . . . "

"I know, Sam. I just — "

"Plus — I don't know if you've thought about this — all the help I could give you with your classes."

"Well, I appreciate —"

"*And,*" Sam continued, stepping closer, "here's another thing. I could introduce you around. To women, Len. And I'm sure you consider Doris rather attractive in her own . . . unique way, but I'm talking gorgeous, my friend. I'm talking —"

"Sam, I'm not going, all right?"

Sam nodded. "Fine," he said quietly. "Just wanted to know

where I stood. Thanks for being honest." He turned and went back to his area.

"And I'm not feeling guilty about it, either," Len added. "You know?"

Sam didn't answer.

"I'm not," Len repeated, and turned to his weeds.

They worked in silence.

Ten minutes passed.

Then the sky cracked overhead, and the air turned suddenly cool. A minute later rain began falling hard in large drops. They continued working.

"Hey!" they heard from across the field, and saw their father standing outside the machine shop a hundred yards away, his welding visor lifted, waving them in.

They began walking through the weeds, heads lowered against the slanting rain.

Len spoke. "I just remembered."

"What."

"Last night. What you said, when you came in."

The rain was quickly thinning into a drizzle.

"Well?"

"You said, 'Len?' You said, 'I'm really glad we'll be working together this summer.' And I said, 'Me too. We'll have some laughs.'" He waited. "'We sure will,' you said. 'A lotta yuks.'" He waited. "Then you started getting kind of sappy, about how lucky you were to have a brother like me, what a good buddy I was, and all this stuff. I guess you were pretty drunk," he added, and waited. "Then you started going on about how sometimes you could be a real asshole. That's how you put it: a real asshole. A total, complete —"

"What about the Shakespeare?" Sam asked.

"What?"

"You said I quoted Shakespeare."

"Yeah, well, you started going, 'Oh, what an asshole, what an asshole am I!'"

Sam gave a short laugh.

Len said, "See? Lotta yuks."

Sam said, "Okay, fine. Wonderful. But I want you to know something, Len. I just want you to know one thing."

"What."

"You're still a complete, absolute, total goddam fool."

"All right."

"I mean it."

"All right."

They walked towards the machine shop where their father stood in the open doorway smoking a cigarette.

18
SWAMI

S am carefully set the needle on the edge of the record. In a moment the first notes of an Indian sitar raga began, low and searching. He turned up the volume just enough to cover the TV out in the living room, where his roommate was watching Saturday morning cartoons with his bacon and eggs. He next lit a match and set the flame to a little black cone of incense in a small gold bowl on his desk. When the flame had caught, he blew out the match, waited a moment, then softly blew out the flame on the incense. Smoke rose, thick and fragrant. He lifted the bowl in both hands and stepped carefully over to the Oriental-looking throw rug on the floor beside his bed and carefully set down the bowl at one end of the rug. A gulping drum had joined the sitar. He took the pillow off his bed, placed it lengthwise in the center of the rug and stood over it, in his robe and socks. Then he slowly brought his palms together in front of his chin, bowed to a poster of the Buddha on the far wall, and recited softly:

> *All beings without number I vow to liberate.*
> *Endless blind passions I vow to uproot.*
> *Dharma gates, beyond measure, I vow to penetrate.*
> *The Great Way of Buddha I vow to attain.*

He knelt over the pillow, straddling it, and doubled it under his buttocks. He cupped his hands in his lap, closed his eyes, and breathed in deeply. Exhaling slowly, he whispered:

"Om mani padme huuummm."

He shifted a little, quickly scratched his nose, and cupped his hands in his lap again.

"Om mani padme huuummm."

There was a knock at the door. "Hey, Swami."

He opened his eyes. "What."

"I'm going to the store. You want anything?"

"No. Nothing."

"Sure?"

"Yes."

Sam waited until he heard the apartment door open and close, then began again.

"Om mani padme huuummm."

Twenty minutes later, when the sitar raga ended, he whispered one more time, with all his concentration: *"Om mani padme huuummm."* Then he stood, a little stiffly, bowed once again to the Buddha, and went to his desk. He sat and opened a notebook; on the cover was carefully printed in large letters: *MEDITATION LOG.* He turned to his last entry, skipped a space and wrote:

October 15

One week today: no cigarettes, coffee, booze, meat, masturbation. Interrupted by Jack at beginning of today's session but did not lose composure. Twice during session began entering perfect silence of mind, but noticed and lost it.

Began using "om mani padme hum" mantra from Tibetan book. May not be pronouncing it correctly. Caught myself fantasizing during session once again about attaining enlightenment and how

I would seem to others, everyone coming for spiritual advice, etc, and became angry with myself, then angry for becoming angry, but finally breathed it all out.

Today's cravings: cigarettes, sex, bacon.

Jack returned, calling out, "Honey, I'm home," then walked with his pounding stride to the kitchen and began noisily putting groceries away.

Sam wrote, *Some people need to make a great deal of noise, whatever they do. Why is that?*

He considered.

He wrote, *Possibly connected with elemental fear of the Great Void.*

Jack stomped up to the door and knocked. "Swami, you decent?"

"Yes."

Jack opened the door and stuck his large red face into the room. "Smells like Good Friday in here."

"Incense."

"Listen, I'm on my way to the high school for some touch football. You want to come?"

"Nah. Thanks, though."

"Come on. We need another guy."

"Some other time. Thanks, though."

Jack gazed around the room. "Where'd you get the poster?"

"Bookstore."

Jack nodded. "The one on Center I always see you hanging around in, right? What's it called?"

"Eastern Light."

"Right." Jack stared over at the poster a moment. "The great Buddha, huh?"

Sam shrugged.

"So what's wrong with good old Jesus Christ?" Jack asked.

"Nothing . . . except Christianity."

"Ah," Jack nodded. "Listen," he said, "I got dish soap."

"All right. My turn, right?"

"Yep."

"I'll get it."

"Good man. See you later."

"Bye."

Jack closed the door. Sam heard him leave the apartment. He wrote: *There is nothing wrong with Christ except Christianity.* He wrote: *Jack has begun calling me "Swami". Have always wanted a nickname. Invited me to play touch football. Said no. Why?*

He sat there a moment. Then he got up and went to the closet for his jeans and sneakers and a sweatshirt.

It was a clear sharp morning, and as he walked through the center of town at a steady, meditative pace, he managed to keep his mind quiet enough to feel himself drawing suddenly closer to this very moment, the eternal Now in which all mystics lived, the stores and people and cars and pale blue sky all becoming wonderfully present to him for a couple of heart beats before he noticed himself having an important experience and the spell was broken.

Excited by this sign of spiritual progress, he took long slow breaths to let his excitement pass, knowing it was his ego that got excited by such notions as "progress," and that was the very thing to get rid of if he wanted to make any real progress.

The Eastern Light bookstore was up at the next corner; he decided to drop in and say hello to Mr Shambava. The strap of little bells on the door jingled cheerfully as he entered.

There was no one around, Mr Shambava probably in his

office, perhaps meditating. The smell of jasmine incense was heavy in the little place, and a tape was quietly playing flute and sitar music. Sam walked around, reading the titles. He loved it in here: the throw rugs on the blond wood floor, the music and incense, and the books: the books all saying there was something to find, a brilliant light inside you, deep inside, under layers and layers of ego. He heard a toilet flush. A few moments later Mr Shambava came walking out through the curtain of beads at the rear of the store, calling out, "Namaste!" He was wearing what Sam still couldn't help thinking of as pyjamas.

"Namaste!" Sam answered, bowing with his palms together.

"May I be of help to you today?" Mr Shambava asked him, walking behind the counter.

"Thank you but no," Sam told him. "I only wish to say hello."

"I see," replied Mr Shambava, cocking his head and smiling with his perfect teeth.

"And are you fine today?" Sam asked.

"Oh, yes. And you?"

"I am fine, also. Yes."

Mr Shambava seemed pleased to hear it.

"I am about to play touch football," Sam told him.

Mr Shambava said, "Ah!"

"An American game," Sam added.

Mr Shambava said, "I hope that you will win."

Sam said, "Thank you. But, of course, what does the *Gita* say?"

"Yes?"

"'Be not moved in success or failure,'" Sam quoted.

Mr Shambava tilted his head and closed his eyes and

nodded. "Of course."

"Don't be attached," Sam added. "Correct?"

"Of course."

"Ego."

"Yes?"

"Get rid of it."

"Sorry?"

"The separate self. The great illusion. Dispose of it, yes?"

Mr Shambava once again closed his eyes and nodded. "Of course."

There was a pause.

"And how is business?" Sam asked.

Mr Shambava shook his head and smiled sadly. "Not extremely well."

Sam nodded. "I'm afraid Americans are not very interested in wisdom, Mr Shambava."

"Perhaps not."

"'Be not moved in success or failure,'" Sam reminded him.

"Of course."

There was another pause.

Sam said, "Well," and brought his palms together. "Namaste."

"Namaste."

Back on the sidewalk he wondered, as he sometimes did, whether Mr Shambava was near enlightenment, or just a friendly guy, or even really a friendly guy. He wondered if Mr Shambava considered him a pest.

Jack and his friends were in the outfield of the high school baseball diamond, trotting around tossing a football to each other. There were five of them.

They need another guy anyway, thought Sam, walking

over. And they didn't look very good: no one had really good moves or hands. Not that it matters, he thought.

Jack saw him and shouted, "Swami! All right!"

Sam lifted his hand.

"Come here, you guys," Jack called to the others.

Ah, don't, Sam thought, walking up.

"Want you to meet my roommate," Jack said to them, as they trotted over. "This is Sam, better known as Swami. Swami, this is Earl the Squirrel, this is Stork Man, this is Elephant, this is Weasel."

Sam nodded back at each, wondering if Jack had given them their nicknames.

"All right." Jack slapped his hands together and rubbed them up. "How about, let's see, me, Swami . . . and Stork Man.

"How's that?"

The others agreed.

"We'll kick." Jack held out his hands for the ball.

As they walked back to kick off, Jack pointed out to Sam the stocking cap, the jacket, the shoes, and the rock for the corners of the field. "Don't let these guys scare you," he added. "It's only touch. I'll let you know what to do."

Sam felt like telling Jack that he was quite far from scared and in fact had probably played as much or more touch football than *he* had — but this was anger, this was ego, and he let the little heat in his chest pass out of him in one long exhalation.

Jack stood holding the ball in position to punt while Sam and Stork Man lined up fifteen yards or so on either side of him. "Gentlemen," he said, looking at Sam, looking at Stork Man, "let's kick some ass."

Stork Man said, "Yo!"

Sam nodded.

Jack took two long strides and punted the ball high and off to the left. The fat guy called Elephant ran under it, waited, dropped it, and Stork Man threw himself on the ball, and was tagged immediately by Weasel.

"All right! Nice job!" shouted Jack, beating his hands together. "Huddle up, gentlemen! Huddle up!"

Sam and Stork Man trotted over.

Jack put his freckled hands on their shoulders and said quietly, "Stork? Line up left, do a stop-and-go. Swami, line up right, go ten yards and cut for the sideline. Let's go!" Walking to the ball Jack announced, "Other team hikes." Sam lined up about ten yards to the right of the ball. Elephant followed him and lined up opposite, one leg forward, hands dangling, looking him in the eye so intensely Sam felt the urge to laugh.

Jack said, "Hike!"

Sam ran up the field, counting his strides, Elephant back-pedalling in front of him, surprisingly quick. At ten Sam cut for the sideline, a step ahead, and looked at Jack, who was gazing downfield, Weasel counting, " . . . thousand four . . . thousand *five*!" Jack heaved the ball, and Sam watched it sail long and high and land a good ten yards beyond Stork Man, who'd gotten clear.

Sam jogged back to where Jack was standing with his hands on his hips, waiting for Stork Man.

"Were you open, Swami?"

"A little."

"Good man."

Stork Man came trotting back on his long legs, shaking his head. "I had him beat."

Jack nodded. "My fault. I thought you could catch up with it."

"Oh, right."

"Thought you had the speed. Sorry."

"Well, shit . . . "

"Okay, shake it off," Jack told him.

They huddled up.

"Stork, same thing, stop-and-go, but when you go I want you to slant left for the corner."

Stork Man nodded.

"Swami, ten yards, cut right. Let's go!"

They lined up.

"Hike!"

Sam bolted ten yards, Elephant with him, took a sharp step to the left, then cut right, wide open, and looked at Jack, who let go with a high, spiralling pass downfield that Stork Man and Earl the Squirrel jumped for together — the ball ticking off their hands and falling behind them.

Returning, Sam whispered, "*Om mani padme huuummm.*"

Stork Man came striding back with his arms spread. "*Lead me a little, will you?*"

"My fault," said Jack. "I thought you could out-jump him."

"Well, I *can* . . . "

"All right, come on, forget it," Jack told him.

They huddled up.

"This time come to a full complete fucking stop, take one step forward and I'll pump-fake. Then you turn and go like a bastard. All right?"

Stork Man nodded.

"Swami, ten yards, cut right. Let's go!"

Sam strolled to the line of scrimmage, arms folded.

"Hike!"

He jogged his ten yards, turned right, jogged towards the out-of-bounds, and watched Jack throw long to Stork Man —

who was wide open and dropped the ball.

Sam tried hard not to be pleased, and in fact looked with attempted compassion at Stork Man, who came marching back with his hands on his hips, barking, "Fuck! *Fuck!*"

As they huddled up, Jack said, "No comment."

Stork Man muttered something.

Jack said, "Pardon me?"

Stork Man didn't repeat it.

"Fourth down, Jack," Weasel sang, spinning the ball up and down.

"We know, we know." Jack put his hand on Sam's shoulder only. "Stork, go long," he said, looking at Sam. "Swami, go ten yards, cut right, head for the sidelines, then cut upfield and I'll hit you. All right, buddy?"

Sam nodded.

Stork Man sighed.

Jack said, "Let's do it!"

Stepping up to the line Sam said quietly, "Om mani padme huuummm."

Elephant said, "What?"

Jack said, "Hike!"

Sam ran, head down, ten yards, Elephant running backwards in front of him. Then he cut right, cut left, cut right again, ran three steps and turned upfield, well ahead of Elephant, and looked over his shoulder towards Jack, who carefully lofted the ball just enough ahead of him, Sam thinking wildly, *Be not moved in success or failure* . . . and he caught the ball in his arms and raced down the field, Jack shouting, "Go, you fucking Swami!"

And as he passed the goal marker he triumphantly flung the ball to the ground — and it bounced straight back in his face against the bridge of his nose. He sank to his knees with his hands over his face, blood running into his mouth.

In his room, Sam sat in bed holding an ice cube in a wash cloth against his nose, staring across at his Buddha poster. The bleeding had stopped but the pain was like a nail.

And as he continued staring at the poster, he noticed for the first time a certain smirk on the full, broad lips. Eyes discreetly lowered, the Buddha seemed to be secretly grinning to himself. And the harder Sam stared, the more intensely held-in-check the Master's mirth appeared—until it seemed that only through his enormous self-control was the great Buddha of Kamakura able to keep from breaking into wild contemptuous laughter.

19
REDBELLY, SLIPPERY JIM AND LIZ

Well, Doris will be pleased. I finally decided on my major.

It happened like this. Today was the first decent day for skating, so after classes I was out there playing hockey and all of a sudden I noticed I was the oldest one on either team. Everyone else was still in high school. Which was real depressing because I remember when I was the *youngest* one, by far. They used to call me The Flea, that's how young. And now here I still was.

I stayed and scored my usual goals, the old wrist shot still there. But afterwards as I left the ice the little play-by-play guy in my head was saying, "Fans, this is a sad day. There he goes. They used to call him The Flea."

I had planned on stopping off at Eddie's, since it's been about a month now, but I didn't. I went home and sat in front of my fish tank, staring at Redbelly, Slippery Jim and Liz, feeling low.

But so was Slippery Jim, the way he was floating kind of cockeyed in a corner. I tapped the glass and he gave a wiggle but that was all. He'd eaten earlier, his color was okay, fins seemed fine. The water looked a *little* murky, so I put all three in a bowl of lukewarm tapwater, got the siphon out and gave the tank a thorough scum sucking, along the walls and the pebble floor and the rock and the castle. And when I poured the three of them back, old Jim took off like a bandit, looking like his slippery self again. So it could have been the water. Or may-be just a mood he was in. Goldfish are hard to figure.

Anyway, *I* felt better, too.

And that's when I decided: Marine Biology. It made a lot of sense. Plus, I liked the sound of it: Len Rossini, marine biologist.

— So, what do you do for a living?
— Me? Oh, I'm a marine biologist.
— How interesting!
— Yes, it is. Very.

What would sound even better, of course, is Len Rossini, Chicago Blackhawks. But like Doris says, "Grow up."

20
ELLEN'S PARTY

Dear Sam,

I am writing this to you instead of coming over and telling it to your face because I do not wish to ever see your face again.

I just want to say that your behavior at my party last night was 1-obnoxious 2-disgusting 3-pathetic 4-a complete embarrassment to me in front of my friends.

I have decided not to send you a bill for the damage to the carpet (1-cigarette burn 2-wine stain which I cannot remove) because, as I said, I want nothing more to do with you — which probably doesn't come as very bad news since you seem to think I and my friends are so "hopeless," as you put it on your way out the door, or I should say as you bellowed it, like some kind of a demented animal.

By the way, talk about hopeless, I heard you out there in the kitchen trying to hustle my best friend Margaret with that bull about how we all have to be naked, completely naked — symbolically speaking, of course. What a line. Also, in case you're interested, Margaret said she found you about as appealing as a worm. That was the exact word she used, a worm. I also couldn't help noticing a pack of cold cuts and a bottle of wine protruding from your coat pockets as you made your dramatic exit. So you're not only a worm, you're a thief too.

I saw it all, Sam.

And do you know what really hurts? I was actually starting to like you a little, maybe even more than a little. I know we'd only been out together three times (four counting the night in the bar that we met, five counting last night, which I don't) but I was beginning to feel that I knew you, and that here was a sensitive and intelligent person. I was even beginning to think that you and I might have a chance at something very special.

But that's all over now. All I can feel for you now, Sam, is 1-pity 2-disgust.

I don't know how much you remember about last night, considering your condition, but do you remember calling my friend David a smug phony asshole? Who you never even *met* before, and who happens to be one of the most sensitive, all-caring people I know, especially for a male, and if you were listening at all to the songs he was playing, which he wrote himself, you might have noticed they deal with issues such as war and social injustice and the necessity for universal brother/sisterhood, and the only reason he wouldn't let you use his guitar was 1- he was in the middle of a song, 2-you were quite obviously plastered. So I guess that gave you the right to start calling him names and then get up and make a *speech* to everyone, with your theme for the evening, how we all need to be naked, down to the skin, down to the bones, down to the *marrow*, shouting and pointing at people, while I'm sitting there wanting to die. To *die*, Sam.

Anyway, just to let you know, you didn't miss anything after you finally left. I was so upset I sent everyone home, everyone but Margaret, thank God for her.

And would you like to hear an interesting opinion of hers, besides the one about you being a worm? (Margaret, by the way, is a straight-A psychology major, please keep that in mind.) She said that beneath all your hyper-aggressive obnoxiousness and this obsession with nakedness, symbolic or not, lies a deep-seated fear of women. And you know what? I agree. I told her about the times we went out and how you never even tried to kiss me except for a quick little peck on the cheek to say goodnight — which I thought at the time was kind of sweet, although I also wondered if you possibly found me somewhat overweight. But now I understand.

I also told her what you said that night in the Hobbit Hole, that no matter what you're doing you're always observing yourself observe yourself observing whatever you're doing, or words to that effect. And she said that is a definite symptom of something very, very psychological.

So as you can see, Sam, I am not just writing to you because I am angry or hurt, although I am, very, and like I said, I do not wish to ever see you again. Not unless 1-you call and arrange to come over so you can do some extremely sincere apologizing, 2-no alcoholic beverages on your person or your breath, and 3-you agree to sit down at some later date with myself and Margaret (this is her idea) and talk, with complete openness and candor, about your present state of mind, which we both agree is rather seriously disturbed, I am sorry to inform you.

If that is too much to ask, then all I can say is I hope you find whatever it is you think you're looking for, although I doubt if you even have any idea. Anyway, maybe along the twisted road of your life you will find someone who is not so hopeless and fat, right? Right.

Ellen

P.S. You left your stocking cap here.

Dear Ellen,

Enclosed is an informal I.O.U. which, as you can see, is made out for the amount of sixty-five dollars. Please accept this as payment for the damage to the carpet and the confiscated wine and cold cuts. I cannot find the words to adequately express my mortification.

Thank you (and Margaret) for the invitation to drop by, but I've decided to withdraw from school and follow that twisted road you mentioned.

You may keep my stocking cap as a memento of our brief but memorable friendship. And let me say right here that I do not regard you as overly fat.

Best of luck with your life, Ellen.

Your pal,
Sam

21
RIGHT STRAIGHT FORWARD
LIKE AN ARROW

I just got off the phone with Doris and I think she's gotten over what happened today. She even agreed that today was all in all a pretty successful one for us at old L and 3C, as we call it. That's for Lewis and Clark Community College where we both go, all the same classes. Today was our first day back after Thanksgiving break and, like I kept telling Doris, a damn successful one, all in all.

I started out almost oversleeping for it, though. My mom finally knocked on the door, but even then I laid there like a bum for another ten minutes. The reason I was so tired, Sam came in from the bar about two in the morning, drunk as a skunk, and shook me awake, saying I was having a nightmare, so he could tell me all over again why he's not going back to school and why he's decided to set out hitchhiking with no destination in mind, just the general direction of Mexico, nakedly experiencing real life, or really experiencing naked life, or something like that. He was still going on when I fell back asleep around three.

I finally got up by telling myself, Three . . . two . . . *one*. I pulled the blanket off my bed and threw it over Sam, partly out of pity and partly just to cover up the sight of him laying there asleep on top of the covers, completely dressed, curled up in a ball like some wino in a doorway.

I took an almost totally cold shower, this being the worst day for me to be tired, with an important speech to deliver, and a crucial quiz in algebra, and a very urgent meeting with my advisor.

I put on my best pants, a white shirt and a tie.

Sam said, "Len." He was curled up under the blanket, head and all, with just his shoes sticking out.

I said, "What." I was working on my tie in front of the mirror.

"Glass of water."

"In a minute."

I finally got the length right and brought him his water and put it on the little table between our beds. "Here."

He came out from under and drank the whole thing down. "Thank you," he said, and went under again.

I put my galoshes on and got my coat and gloves and books.

"Len?"

"What."

"Close the door when you leave."

My mom had Cream of Wheat and juice and bacon ready for me.

She sat across the table with a cup of coffee and a cigarette.

"Who was the water for? Him?" she said, keeping her voice down.

I nodded, breaking my bacon into the Cream of Wheat, kind of weird, I know.

"I heard the two of you talking last night," she said.

"You heard *him*."

"So what's going on? Did he tell you?"

"Just that stuff about wanting to hitch-hike around."

"Why, though? Did he say?"

"Not really."

"Did something happen at school? A girl or something?"

"I don't think so."

"Well, what do you think it *is*, then?

"I don't know, Mom."

All that stuff about being naked, I wasn't going to tell her that. By the way, speaking of naked, little did I know — but I'll get to that later.

"I guess he just has this travel bug," I said.

"But to drop out of school, after doing so well . . . "

"I know."

She watched me eat.

"Good bacon," I said. "Just right."

"Is he really going to do this, Len? Do you think?"

"What, go hitchhiking?"

"Yes."

"Well, probably not today."

Sam's been leaving the next day ever since he got in last week.

"Your father . . . " She shook her head and took a drag on her cigarette.

Doris honked.

I got up and slugged down the rest of my juice.

"Oh for God sakes, take it easy," my mom said.

"I *am*." I took my coat very leisurely off the back of the chair and very leisurely put in on.

"Can't she come to the door?" my mom said. "I think that's so ignorant, honking for people."

"Well, with the snow," I said, which was kind of lame because Doris *always* just honks. It's partly because she thinks my mom doesn't like her, which I guess is true. My mom thinks she's too bossy.

"Go, before she leaves without you."

"Ah, she wouldn't do that." I was taking my time putting on my gloves, even though I hate making people wait for me, especially Doris. But I didn't want to look whipped in front of my own mother. So it was kind of a spot.

Doris honked again.

"Len, go."

"All right." I grabbed my books. "Bye."

"Goodbye."

It was pretty outside, everything covered and the snow still falling.

Doris scooted over and I got in behind the wheel. I've had my license for about two weeks now. Doris trained me for it.

"Good morning, darling!" she said. "Isn't it lovely?"

Ever since we got engaged last month she's been talking like that, calling me "darling". I know she gets it from those Masterpiece Theatre things on public TV she's always watching.

I kept my foot on the brake pedal while I shifted the gear stick from park into drive, then slowly pressed my foot on the gas and we moved away.

This was my first time driving in weather like this and I would have to say I did pretty good, even with Doris instructing me every foot of the way, and when we got to school I found a spot along a side street and parallel-parked that sucker perfectly.

"Excellent, darling."

"Elementary."

Our first class was Speech 100, *my* speech scheduled first.

All the way to the building Doris kept saying things like, "Don't be nervous, darling. Just remember, I'll be out there," and by the time we got to class I was ready to bolt.

I did really good, though. Didn't read from my three-by-five cards except for the quote from Nixon, good eye contact, expressive use of the hands, especially where I pounded on the lectern at one point to show strong conviction, and at the very end I put something special into my voice while I said in conclusion, "So! Let us not feel defeated! Let us instead feel happy and glad and joyful that our boys are coming back home!" Then I said, "Thank you," and returned to my desk.

Doris leaned over and whispered, "You were *won*derful."

The guy up next did a rebuttal. This was our persuasive assignment and Dr Lane put us all in pairs, pro and con, and this guy I was put with, Gary Baker, has a cousin in the Green Berets, so we decided he'd be for the continuation of the war and I'd be glad it's ending, which I am.

"Ladies and gentlemen," he said. "I had a speech very carefully written out." He held up his three-by-five cards. "But you know what?" he said, and tried to tear them up. Only trouble, he's this real fat, soft-looking guy and he couldn't do it. A couple people laughed and he threw the cards on the floor and started telling us very loudly about his cousin Billy in the Green Berets and how he wished to God he didn't have this problem with his weight which was not from overeating but a glandular condition or else he'd be *out* there, fighting side by side with Billy. Then he took out a hankie and wiped his forehead, calming down, and started talking about the strategic importance of Vietnam. Which got a little boring and I started thinking about me and Sam, how we used to play Marines, him being Sarge, me the kid. Then I thought about him probably still in bed now, curled up under the blanket with his shoes sticking out . . . .

All of a sudden Baker banged his fist on the lectern and started shouting again: "And why? Because I'm an American! Proud of it! And proud of my cousin Billy!" Then he pointed at me. "But it's people like this, cowards like this, that make . . . me . . . *sick.*"

I was surprised. He seemed so shy before, when we talked together about our topics.

Anyway, when he pointed at me and said I made him sick, everyone looked where he pointed and I couldn't help lowering my head, which probably made me look ashamed. And then Doris, just to complete the scene, reaches over for my arm and says in her loudest whisper, "Don't listen to him, darling. You're *not* a coward."

"And let me just say in closing," Baker goes, "God bless the Green Berets. God bless my cousin Billy." Then in a loud, choking voice: "And God bless the United States of America!"

Some of the people in the class applauded, including, for a clap or two, Doris.

I looked at her.

"I was thinking of Donald," she said.

Donald's her brother. He's a career man in the Coast Guard. Did a lot of fighting out there in Lake Michigan.

Dr Lane asked Baker to pick up his three-by-five cards from the floor, which he did.

The next two speeches were on the bottle return issue.

After class Doris thought I should go up to Baker and tell him to take back what he said about me being a coward. I didn't feel like it, though. It was just a speech, and anyway I knew I'd done a pretty good job myself, possibly a B, which would be great because I'm right in the middle of a B and a C in that class.

"Or *are* you a coward?" she goes.

Baker wasn't too far ahead of us in the hallway and I said, "Hey, Gary?"

He stopped and turned around. He looked pretty nervous.

I came up to him, Doris on my arm. "I'm not a coward," I said, "okay?"

He nodded. "Okay."

"I have a brother in the Coast Guard," Doris added, for whatever that was worth.

He nodded.

Then we all just stood there.

"Well," he said, "I better get to class," and walked off.

Doris shook her head. "Look at the butt on him."

Almost all the classes and offices at L and 3C are in one big building, Douglas Hall, where we were, so we got to algebra early enough for me to look over the day's unit one more time, real quick, and to ask Doris a couple of questions — she's a brain in math. And I think I really tore up on the quiz he gave us, which could bring me up to a very solid C, possibly a C +.

So I was feeling pretty good for my meeting right afterwards with my advisor, Dr Rosenthal. Doris said she'd be at our booth in the student center and I gave her my books and took the stairs to room 324, a little nervous. I'd never met the guy before. I made the appointment over the phone.

The door was open and this guy that looked a lot like Eric Nesterinko, who used to play right wing for the Blackhawks, was sitting at his desk putting a new ribbon into his typewriter.

I said, "Dr Rosenthal?"

"Come in," he said, without looking up.

I walked right over to his desk and put out my hand and said, "Sir, I'm Leonard Rossini."

That's the way to be, you know? Right straight forward like an arrow.

Except, he didn't look up. "Have a seat," he said. "Be right with you."

I had a seat.

"There," he said, and closed the typewriter lid. "So. What can I do for you?"

Now he looked even more like Eric Nesterinko.

I explained the reason I was there: to find out what classes he would recommend while I'm here at L and 3C, in order to prepare for the University the year after next, where my major, I've now decided, is going to be marine biology. I said it like that, all in one sentence.

He leaned way back — he had one of those chairs — and put his hands behind his head and looked up at the ceiling, exactly what I would have done in his place, with my own office, people coming to see me for advice. He told the ceiling I should get my general requirements out of the way while I'm here and worry about my major when I get to the University. Then he asked me what I was hoping he would: Why marine biology?

I tried to make my answer sound like it wasn't memorized. "Sir," I said, "ever since I was a very small child I have always had an interest and, well, *fond*ness for fish, always keeping two or three goldfish on hand, and I would very much enjoy, well, broadening my knowledge and understanding of other aquatic creatures and, well, underwater life in general."

He nodded, still sitting way back, and kind of smiled a little. Which *might* have meant, This is good to see—a young man who knows where he's going and why. Or else it could have meant, Goldfish, what a stupid reason to choose your major.

Then all of a sudden he sprang forward, folded his hands on top of his typewriter and said, "Anything else?" Which I figured meant, I'm very busy, no time for people majoring in Goldfish. He was looking a lot less like Eric Nesterinko, who was always a gentleman, on the ice and off.

I stood up and said, "No, I believe that's it."

But then *he* stood up and put out his hand and said, "What was the name again?"

"Rossini, sir." We shook each other's hand. "Leonard Rossini."

"Well, Mr Rossini, I'm sure you'll do fine," he said, "just fine."

"Thank you, sir. Thank you very much," I said to him. "And thanks for your help."

"Anytime," he said — in other words, drop by anytime.

"Bye, sir."

"So long."

I could feel him thinking as I walked out the door: Now *there's* a young man who knows where he's going.

Outside, the snow was still coming down, heavy as ever. There was no one around, everyone in their classes, and it was very quiet. I put up my collar and headed towards the student center, where Doris was waiting. I was looking forward to telling her about my meeting with Dr Rosenthal and how well it went.

It was so quiet, though.

And as I walked along I started doing this thing I used to do as a kid—looking straight up into the falling snow. It gives you a very unusual effect, like absolutely everything is gone, including the ground and the sky, with nothing but the snow coming down . . . down . . . down . . . and I stumbled against a snowbank and snapped out of it.

Doris was at our usual booth in the Lincoln Lounge, reading the school paper and smoking one of her skinny, footlong cigarettes. She started smoking about the time she started calling me darling. She doesn't inhale, so I guess it's all right.

She looked up and saw it was me and smiled.

I smiled, too.

I sat beside her and told her about my meeting with Dr Rosenthal. She listened, but towards the end she was waiting for me to finish, because as soon as I did she gave my hand a squeeze and said, "I have something to show you."

"What."

"About a band."

"Oh."

She meant a band for our wedding reception at the Ramada Inn, in June. First it was going to be her uncle Bill's band, The Merry Beer Barrels, but that would be entirely polkas, which worried her. So then it was this local rock band she'd heard was pretty good, called the Lavender Machine, but we went to hear them and the lead singer kept acting like he was having an orgasm. So then she swung all the way in the other direction and wanted to find a little group of violin players in tuxedos doing classical music, but I talked her out of that. Anyway, now she had the answer to our prayers, as she put it, right there in the student paper classifieds.

"'The Majestics,'" she read, "'music from Sinatra to Santana,'" and looked at me.

"I think we got a winner," I said.

Actually, I wish we could just have a nice little church service instead of a whole Mass, even though we're both Catholic, and then everyone go to a good expensive restaurant like Antonio's or something, pull some tables together, and let it go at that.

She got her pen from her purse and circled the ad. Then she put her hands on mine and looked at me and said how happy she was.

"Me, too," I said.

"Five and a half months," she said, meaning how long before the wedding.

"Boy," I said.

We don't have the money for a honeymoon but her parents have a cottage up in Michigan with a boat and she's going to teach me to water ski. Then we're going to rent an apartment and get part-time jobs and keep going to L and 3C, saving every penny we can, eating a lot of soup, and then get married-couple housing at the University. No kids until we finish school and I start my career as a marine biologist, Doris working too, possibly as a math teacher or a television weather lady, until she gets too pregnant. If it's a boy we're naming it Donald after her brother and if it's a girl we're naming it Samantha after Sam.

We're already training ourselves to go without lunch, so we sat there holding hands and talking about the future until it was time for English class.

All we did today was discuss this book we had to finish reading over break, *The Sun Also Rises* by Ernest Hemingway, born in Oak Park, Illinois in 1899, died in Ketchum, Idaho in 1961, by suicide with a shotgun and I can see why. What a depressing writer.

Participation in class discussions counts for twenty per cent of our grade so I raised my hand and said something about what a vivid description of the bullfights, but that was it.

Outside after class the snow had finally stopped. The sidewalks were mostly clear but Doris was holding on tight to my arm, as if to keep from falling. Sometimes she likes to play the weaker sex. So I started carrying on, kind of big and mad, about books like *The Sun Also Rises*, and for God sakes let's have some books that *inspire* us. I couldn't think of any offhand, not being much of a reader, but I kept going on like that, and by the time we got to the car she was hanging all over me.

Her car looked like something in a bakery window. I brushed off the license plate in the back just to make sure it said DOLLY. The car's from her dad for graduation last year and that's what he calls her. She's a real daddy's girl.

Anyway, we got in and I started the engine and turned on the heater full blast and began climbing all over looking for the scraper, which she couldn't remember what she did with.

All the time I was looking she kept going on about how cozy it was in the car, with the heater warming up and all the windows covered with snow, completely covered, nobody able to see inside, to see what we might be *doing* inside . . . .

I looked at her. She gave me this little smile.

Doris has a thing about sex in places where we might get caught. One time we did it in my room with my mother in the kitchen on the phone.

Anyway, we got undressed, right there in the car, which

we've done before, but not along a side street a block from school in daylight. We threw everything in the back as we took it off. The only thing I kept wearing was my watch and the only thing she kept wearing was her engagement ring. Then she laid along the seat, reached up her arms and said, "Take me, darling."

So I settled in.

We were going along very, very nicely. She was calling me every sweet thing in the world. And then she let out a scream.

I pulled back. "What'd I *do*?"

She curled herself up against the seat and yelled, "Drive!"

I finally noticed. The windshield wipers were going — she must have accidentally flipped them on with her foot — and the windows were clear, and two guys were leaning over the hood on the passenger side, grinning in.

"Drive!"

"I am!"

But first I had to open and close my door as hard as I could to knock some snow off the window and the side view mirror, then put the car in reverse and back up very slowly until I felt it nudge the car behind us, then shift into forward, keeping my foot on the brake while I turned the wheel as far as I could, then flip on the turning signal, check my window for traffic behind us, and carefully pull out — do all that while Doris is screaming "Drive!" and those two grinning assholes are watching.

I decided right away where to go. There's this place for picnics and barbecues where we sometimes go to park at night. It's kind of dangerous, gangs and such, but not now, daytime and the weather, and we could put our clothes on in peace.

Doris wouldn't even get in the back but just laid there

curled up against the seat in a little whimpering naked ball. I tried to say comforting stuff but most of my mind was on driving, being new, plus the road conditions, plus I'm bare naked, driving a naked girl, and all we needed was to get in an accident.

L and 3C is between our town and this very depressing town called Morton, and the park is on the other side of Morton, towards the city, so I had to drive through Morton.

What a town. Half the stores are boarded up and the ones still open are mostly liquor stores or dirty movie houses or a grubby-looking laundromat, and whatever the weather you'll always see these really depressing-looking people walking around — bag ladies and prostitutes and winos — who don't even know how lost and aimless they are. And like Doris says: How can people let themselves *get* like that?

We hate driving through that town, even fully dressed.

Luckily I only had to stop for one red light.

Doris said, "Are we there?"

"Almost," I said, and put my hand on her leg.

"Don't touch me!"

We finally reached the park and I pulled into the lot and left the car running.

"Okay, Dee."

She climbed into the back and started pulling on her clothes and tossing mine up front — along with, guess what, the scraper.

"Where was it?" I said.

No answer.

We got dressed. I even put my tie back on. It felt so good and human wearing clothes again.

I got out with the scraper and did the rest of the windows.

She was still in the back, sitting there with her arms folded. I tapped on her window. She looked and I winked and she looked away.

Back inside the car I said, "Dee, come on up, okay?"

"No."

"Come on. You're all right."

She looked out her window.

"You want me to come back there?"

"No."

"You want to go home?"

"No." She started crying again.

"I'm coming over," I said.

"No!"

I sat back down.

At least we had a pleasant view: some trees with all their branches holding snow, and a snow-covered picnic table with a bunch of sparrows hopping all over it.

I had a very pleasant thought while sitting there. I said, "Dee, you know what?" I waited. I said, "Dee?"

"What."

I said, "Someday we're going to laugh about this little experience today. We'll be sitting together on the couch, in our own little place, the kids are in bed, little Donald and Samantha..." I checked the rear view mirror. She was looking out her window. I went on. "And you'll say, 'Darling, remember that time in the old Dodge Dart —'"

"You should've got out and kicked their ass," she said.

"Dee, I wasn't even dressed."

"If we were *dressed* they wouldn't have been looking."

I could have mentioned whose idea getting naked was, but I didn't.

"You should have smashed their smiling . . . fucking

. . . faces."

At least she was talking again.

"If I ever see them again, Dee, I will."

"Sure."

"No, I really will. I'll make them sorry, Dee. I'll hurt them bad."

"Promise?"

"I promise. Now come on up, all right?"

She gave a sigh and started climbing over. "What will you do if you see them?" She sat by the door.

"Come here and I'll tell you."

"No. What will you do?"

"Dee, I'll tear them limb from limb, okay?"

"Be serious, please."

I told her I would hit them as hard as I possibly could. I looked at my fists, one and the other, and said I wished the sonofabitches were here right now.

She scooted over. "What would you do? Describe it."

I put my arm around her and she snuggled against me while I told her what I would do. I had them both on the ground, holding them by the hair and cracking their heads together, calling them every filthy thing I could think of, and she put her tongue in my ear, which drives me wild, and we started going at it. After about a minute I was pushing up her skirt but she said very definitely, "No." I didn't argue and we went back to just cuddling, which was nice, the snow on the trees, the sparrows on the picnic table, my future wife in my arms.

"Promise me something?" she said.

"What."

"Promise me you won't go after those guys? They're not worth it, darling. And I'm afraid of how you get."

Afraid I'd go too far and kill them, she meant. Which is one of our little ideas about me, that I'm very, very dangerous when I get truly angry.

I said, "I don't know, Dee. Seems like they should have to pay, you know?"

"Darling, please? Please promise me you won't go after them?"

I gave a big sigh. "All right. I promise."

"Thank you."

"I still say —"

"Darling, no."

"All right."

"Kiss me."

I did.

"I love you so much," she said.

"Me too. I mean I love you, too."

"Let's go home now," she said.

I drove all the way home with only one hand on the wheel and my arm around her shoulder while we talked — mostly me — about the way I know it's going to be if we just keep moving forward, right straight forward like an arrow.

I didn't even notice driving through Morton.

I was still talking when I pulled up in front of my house, but she cut me off:

"Your brother."

Sam was standing in the front room window with his hands in his bathrobe pockets, watching us.

"Bye," she said.

Doris and Sam don't like each other at all.

"Call me," I said.

"All right."

I got out and she scooted over and drove away. I forgot my books but I'll see her tomorrow.

I waved hi to Sam at the window.

He nodded his head, kind of slow, like saying yes, I see you, and like it made him sad, what he saw. Sad and kind of disgusted. Or maybe not, I don't know. Maybe it was just his hungover face.

Anyway, I made a snowball and walked to the window, went into a pitcher's wind-up, and threw it at him. But he just kept looking at me, with that face.

So I did a little humorous thing, pretending like I couldn't stand it, the way he was looking at me, looking *into* me, and I put out my hands in front of my face and shook my head, like saying *No . . . please . . . no*, and sank to my knees, looking into those eyes, and spread my arms and fell on my face in the snow, stone dead, and laid there.

Then I looked up. But he'd gone.

I laid my head back down. I felt so tired all of a sudden. I felt like I could sleep right there in the snow, no problem. I thought, *Get up, you bum*. But I didn't. I thought, *Three . . . two . . . one*, and still laid there. I tried it again: *Three . . . two . . . one*, and got up.

22
FLEDGLING

Sunday, December 2

Mom, Dad, Len,

By the time you return from church and find this, I hope to be well on my way.

I sincerely wish to apologize for my moodiness these past two weeks among you. The only excuse I can offer is this: I was waiting for a voice in my soul to say, "Now. Now is the time. Spread your wings and fly."

That voice has finally spoken.

When will I return? Difficult to say. Possibly not for years. But I will return. Perhaps as a prince, perhaps as a pauper. Hopefully, as a wiser man.

Until then, I remain —

Your loving son/brother,
Sam

23

THE ROSSINI BROTHERS

It was my mom who told me about Eddie. I was back from classes having a sandwich at the kitchen table when she came in from grocery shopping. I asked her if she got any jelly but she didn't answer. She just set the bag on the counter top and came over.

"What's the matter?" I said.

She sat at the table. "I have some bad news, hon."

"What."

"It's about Eddie."

I waited.

She said, "He got hit by a car this morning, on his bike . . . and he died, hon."

I got up from the table and went to my room.

I fed my fish. Then I got out my hockey stick, even though it's spring, and started putting fresh tape on the blade.

She tapped on the door. "Len?"

I said, "Mom, I'm real busy right now, okay?"

"All right. I'll be out in the kitchen."

When I finished with my stick I made my bed. Then I looked around. I couldn't find anything else so I pulled off the blanket and sheet and started making the bed again. Then I couldn't. I sat on the floor.

The wake was at Crawford's Funeral Home, in Morton. My dad said I could borrow his car, but Doris insisted on coming too, so we took hers. She wanted to help me through this. That's how she put it. She wouldn't even let me drive. She said I was still in a mild state of shock.

Eddie's mom was a mess. She was sitting in a chair with a couple of men around her, probably Eddie's uncles, but they weren't making any difference. I didn't even go over to her.

They had him in an open casket. I went up there with Doris on my arm. It was him all right. He was wearing the blue suit he always wore to Mass, with the skinny red tie with little horseshoes down it. His hair was combed very carefully. I stood there looking at his long bony face with orange makeup all over it and even some lipstick. I kept trying to pray, to at least say one Hail Mary.

Then I noticed Doris, boo-hooing away, and I took my arm back and headed down the aisle and outside into the parking lot and kept walking, Doris hurrying after me, going "Len . . . ? Len . . . ?"

She finally caught up, and I stopped.

"Where you *going*?" she said.

I didn't answer. I wouldn't even look at her. I just stood there with my arms folded, looking away.

"Let's get you into the car," she said, and took my arm.

I yanked it away. "Why are *you* here?" I said to her.

"Len . . . "

"No, really. You never even liked him," I said. "You didn't even want me hanging around with him. He was a *re*tard."

"I never called him that."

"But you know what?" I said. "I liked him a thousand times better than I like you. 'Cause you know why? 'Cause you're a bitch."

She slapped me.

I slapped her back.

She slugged me with her fist, knocking me back a little, then stepped up and kneed me straight in the balls. I went down. She sobbed at me, "I'm sorry!" and ran to her car. I heard her get in and drive away.

This was the second time since I've known Doris that she kneed me in the balls. The first time was mostly an accident, though. Anyway, I was down on all fours breathing long and deep, the way you should. Then some old guy and his wife on the way to their car stopped and asked if I was all right. They might have been Eddie's grandparents, now that I think about it. I told them I was looking for my contact lens. They were going to start helping me look so I said, "Here it is," and lifted my finger and put it against my eye.

"Shouldn't you wash it first?" the lady asked.

"Nah," I said. Then I tried standing up. "Bad back," I told them.

"You're bleeding," the man said, pointing at my face.

Doris is left-handed — left-*fisted* — and that's the hand her engagement ring is on, which cuts pretty good. It should. It cost me enough.

I wiped my cheek bone and looked at my hand. "Oh," I said, "thanks," and walked away. I could feel them watching me, probably shaking their heads.

I didn't feel like walking all the way home, and didn't feel like going home anyway, so I decided to go to Sam's. He's got an apartment in Morton not very far from the funeral home. He wouldn't be back from work for another hour or so — he works at a Seven-Eleven on the other side of Morton — but I had a key. He agreed to let me use the place now and then for sex with Doris, as long as we only use the floor, with our own blanket, and as long as we're gone before he gets home. He hates Doris.

This was my first time ever in Morton on foot. It's a pretty rough town, very down and out, and mostly black. So, being white and wearing a suit and tie, I got some looks. Or maybe they were just reacting to the blood on my face. I was wishing I had a handkerchief.

Only three people actually said anything. One was this black kid sitting on the hood of a car outside a laundromat. "Boy, what the fuck *you* doing here?" he said in this voice real high and fast.

I didn't answer. He was just a kid, being tough. And anyway it was a good question.

Then a few blocks later along a side street this woman's voice goes, "Who cut *you* up?"

I looked. She was sitting on a stoop outside the doorway of an apartment building, eating from a little bag of potato chips. She was black but her hair was gold and she had a low-cut silky dress on, with big huge boobs and arms, a big huge butt, and a big round face with a big red mouth. She wasn't fat, just massive.

I stopped and answered her question. "My fiancée," I said.

She laughed over that, this little tee-hee laugh with the tip of her tongue between her teeth, her eyelids drooping, knockers bobbing. "You still gonna marry this woman?"

Good question.

I said, "Nah."

"Well, *thass* good," she said. "'Cause you're real sweet-looking."

I didn't know what to say to that so I shrugged.

"You wanna come upstairs with me, honey? I'll fix you up."

She meant the cut on my face but more than that too.

I looked at her straight and said, "Sure."

"Cost you some money." She put a potato chip in her mouth.

I had no idea how much a prostitute usually costs — I'd never even talked to one before — but I knew three dollars and some change wasn't even close. I wanted her to take me up there really bad, though. It wasn't horniness. In fact, my balls were still feeling pretty sore and useless.

I asked if I could owe her the money.

That gave her another tee-hee. "You come back some other time," she said.

I tried to think. "I could give you my driver's license, to hold till I paid you." Which I knew would be an unusual arrangement, but I just wanted so bad to go up there and get lost in her, just get totally lost in her.

"You come back some other time," she said again, but without laughing.

I didn't want to beg. "Couldn't I just —"

"Run along now, honey. Go on. Before I get mad."

I said, "All right," and ran along.

"Bye, honey."

I walked to the end of the block and went left down another sorry-looking side street. Then this very skinny guy in a greasy bowling jacket, a white guy, came running up out of nowhere, holding something pointed in his jacket pocket, going, "Hey!"

I stopped.

"Give me a dollar, man, or I'll kill you, I swear to fucking God," he said.

I couldn't tell what he had in his pocket, a very little gun or his finger, but either way he didn't even scare me, the mood

I was in. I wanted to show him how much he didn't scare me, but the way he was standing there, shaking all over, I thought to hell with it and took out my wallet and gave him all three of my dollars. He grabbed it and backed away, hand in his jacket, still keeping me covered.

I finally got to Sam's.

It's on the third floor in an old brick apartment building. The stairway smells like piss and puke and there's all this angry stuff spray-painted on the walls. My folks have been there once, right after he moved in. My dad said my mom started crying a little on the way up.

The apartment isn't bad at all, though. He's got a little kitchen with a little bathroom off it and a little front room with a couch that opens out into a bed. He keeps the place pretty clean.

Soon as I got in I started walking all around, looking for something to make me stop seeing Eddie in his casket. I ended up in front of a calendar on the kitchen wall that had a self-portrait of Vincent Van Gogh, the guy who cut off his ear. I gave him a good long look. He definitely appeared to be someone who could cut off his own ear. He didn't look crazy, though. He just had this look like there was something very basically wrong, and like there wasn't anything he could do about it, except maybe cut off his ear.

The phone rang, on the wall by the door.

It was my mom. She figured I was here. She said Doris had called, looking for me.

I said, "Okay. Thanks."

"How you doing, mister?"

"All right. I'm just waiting for Sam."

She told me to call if I wanted to come home later and she'd pick me up.

I said okay, but I'd probably be staying.

She told me to eat something.

I said I would. "I'll see you later," I said, "okay?"

"All right."

"Bye," I said.

"Bye, hon."

I hung up the phone and it rang. I picked it up and said hello and Doris said, "Len?"

I said, "Hi."

She started crying in my ear. She said she was sorry for leaving me there like that. She said she got home and turned right around and came back but I was gone. She said she drove up and down, looking. She asked me if I meant it when I called her a bitch.

I told her no.

She asked me if I still loved her.

I told her yes. I just wanted to get off.

She asked me if I still wanted to marry her.

I said, "Fine."

"*Fine?*"

"I mean yes, I want to marry you. Okay?"

She went on then, about our "relationship," all the ins and outs of it. Between her and her mom they get about fifty different women's magazines a month.

She went on for quite a while, but I wasn't listening. I was remembering the one and only time she met Eddie. It was her idea. We'd had this fight. I think it was the one where she called Sam a Communist. Anyway, when we got back together after a couple of days she thought it would be good for our relationship if she got to meet Eddie, since he was my best friend. I liked the idea. I figured maybe after she met him she'd see what an interesting and funny and excellent guy he was and quit thinking of him as someone I was being friends with out of charity.

It didn't work out, though.

I remember his mom let us in and said he was in the basement, go on down, and as we went downstairs I could hear the trains. Eddie has this unbelievable – *had* this unbelievable H.O. train set covering practically half the entire basement floor, with little towns and crossings and tunnels and stations and people and trees and three long trains — two freights and a passenger. But even though I'd already told Doris about the train set, about how complicated it was to run and how it wasn't like a kid thing at all, still I wished he was doing something else.

He was kneeling over his control box and started to smile, but seeing Doris behind me his face went tight, and I said real fake and loud, "Eddie! Hey! Want you to meet somebody! This is Doris!"

He said, "Hi," and went back to working the levers and buttons on his control box. But Doris — she puts out her arms and looks all around the floor, going "Wow! Leonard told me you had a big train set, but my goodness!"

Eddie didn't even look at her but just kept working at keeping the trains snaking around, only faster. He was a wizard with that control box.

Meanwhile, Doris goes walking on her tip-toes between the tracks and gets right down on her knees beside him. "Boy," she says, "that looks really complicated!"

I'm still standing by the stairs and Eddie looks over at me like saying "What the hell is *this*?"

I just shrugged like saying "Beats me."

Doris says, "I really *like* trains. You don't mind if I watch — do you, Eddie?"

He didn't answer. He just kept the trains going a little bit faster and faster, Doris kneeling there beside him, shaking her head in amazement at how smart he was for an idiot.

Then, for the first time I ever saw it happen, two of the trains came together at a junction and, instead of at the last split second taking different tracks, they ran straight into each other, both of the engines rearing up and a line of boxcars flying off and rolling over into a church, wiping out all the members of a wedding standing out front.

Doris said real quiet, "Oh, gosh."

Eddie looked at her. He was breathing in and out kind of hard.

"Len?" she said, getting up. She came walking over in a hurry, stepping all over the tracks. I told her to go on, and she went up the stairs and out.

Eddie was sitting there staring at the mess in front of the church. I tried to lighten him up: "Got any ambulances?"

"Get out of here," he said, still staring at the church.

I said, "Hey, come on."

He looked at me. "Get out!"

So I did.

Doris was waiting for me out in the driveway. There was a big huge yellow moon, I remember. She came up and threw her arms around me and started crying, hard. I held her and said things, but I kept worrying about Eddie or his mom seeing us out there like that.

Then we got in her car — her mom's car — and Doris drove to "our place," as we called it, the parking lot at Carver Park, on the other side of Morton, where we always went to make out. But this time when we got there she was different. This time she didn't stop my hands at all. In fact, hers were just as busy and we ended up completely naked, both of us breathing like mad. Then it took some maneuvering but she was finally straddling my lap, and God almighty, I was hers and she was mine, looking straight in each other's eyes.

And meanwhile Eddie was probably riding all over town on his bike as hard as he could, the way he always did whenever he was bothered by something a lot, the way he was probably riding when he got hit.

Anyhow, I was thinking back on all that, and then Doris on the phone said, "Well?"

I said, "Well what."

She said, "Is it yes or no?"

I decided right then and there. I said, "It's no, Dee."

She didn't speak for a moment. Then she said, "Well . . . I guess there's *some* hope for us."

I should have found out what she'd actually asked me before I answered.

"Wouldn't you say?" she added.

"I guess. Listen, I have to go now."

"Can I see you tonight?" she said.

I told her I'd be staying over with Sam.

She sighed. "Well, will you please call me tomorrow?"

I told her I would, and got off.

I went back to walking all around, opening and closing stuff — his refrigerator, the cupboards, the closet. I'm not usually a snoop but I just wanted to stop thinking about things, at least for a while.

The only interesting thing I found was this big manila envelope on the shelf in the closet, full of letters. I brought it over to the couch.

Most of them were from me, a few from my mom, one from a guy named Jack who wanted forty dollars Sam owed him — he kept calling Sam "Swami". And a long one from a girl named Ellen, all about Sam's behavior at her party. It sounded like he'd been leaning pretty far over the deep end. The letter was postmarked November fourteenth, just before he came home for Thanksgiving and didn't go back, and it made me think how much I'd hardly talked to him since he was home, except listening half asleep when he came in drunk a couple times, and then he took off somewhere for a week and when he came back he got this apartment and I hardly even saw him anymore. Anyway, other stuff in there—a postcard from my parents' trip to Florida last year, in my dad's handwriting, everything ending in an exclamation point. And a little notebook, with a couple of weird poems and about ten different versions of a note he left for me and my parents when he took off last December, all about hearing a voice and spreading his wings and not coming back for years. He was only gone, like I said, about a week or so. I don't know what happened. I've asked him but he never wants to talk about it. And like I said, we haven't talked much lately anyway.

That was it and I put everything back and went looking around for something else, gave up and turned on the little TV my folks bought him, on the coffee table. I watched a couple minutes of a *Star Trek* I'd already seen, and turned it off, and ended up looking through his collection of books lined up on the floor along the wall. I actually ran across one that belonged to me, called *Crime and Punishment*, by Fyodor Dostoevski. Sam gave it to me about four or five Christmases ago but I never read it, just the first chapter, because it seemed too gloomy and boring. I brought it over to the couch and tried it again.

I reread the whole first chapter without even stopping. It

was still gloomy but it wasn't boring, not at all. I got up for a pee before chapter two.

Then, just as I was about to leave the bathroom, all of a sudden it hit me: Eddie was dead and I would never see him again. Ever.

Maybe Doris was right about me being in a mild state of shock or something, because this was the first time it really and truly came through. I shoved my face in my arms against the door and started crying like I'd just found out.

But almost right away I heard Sam's key at the apartment door, to the kitchen, and I stopped so hard I almost choked. I grabbed a towel and wiped my eyes and checked in the mirror to see if you could tell. You could, but I figured so what?

I didn't come out, though. I don't know why except I guess it gave me some kind of stupid little kick to be in there listening to Sam while he thought he was alone.

I heard him put something down that sounded like a grocery bag. Then he walked to the living room, slow and shuffly like his shoes were too big, and opened the colset door—hanging up his jacket, I guess. He closed the door and shuffled back to the kitchen. I heard him putting groceries away. The phone rang. He went on putting stuff away. It kept ringing and he finally answered it.

"Hello . . . No, he's not . . . Well, he's not here now . . . No idea." He hung up.

Doris.

I heard him get a pan or something and bring it over to the stove. Then I started feeling too creepy doing this. So I flushed the toilet. "That *you* out there, Sam?" I said.

He didn't answer.

I came out, hitching my pants. "I wouldn't go in there for

a while," I warned.

He stood there by the stove, looking at me. Then he went back to opening a can. "You scared me," he said. He didn't seem very shook, though. He didn't seem very *anything*.

I leaned against the wall by the stove and watched him dump a can of chicken chow mein into the pan.

"Sorry about Eddie," he said, turning the flame full blast.

I nodded.

"I was going to call you tonight," he said.

I nodded.

"Anyway . . . sorry."

I nodded some more. I was afraid if I used my voice it would come out crying.

"Where'd you get the cut?" he said, stirring up his slop.

"Doris."

"What'd she do, knife you?"

"Punched me, with her ring on."

He shook his head.

"Then, after that —"

"That was her, by the way, on the phone."

"I know. Then she kneed me, straight in the balls."

He turned the burner down.

"This is in the parking lot, right outside the *funeral* home," I told him.

He shook his head again, clicked his tongue, and told me to get a couple plates and forks from the dish rack.

I got them. "Then she just *left*," I said, setting the table, "just —"

"There's napkins in the cupboard over the sink."

"Just got in her car and drove away," I said. I got the napkins.

I wanted him to say how much he hated her. Then I would

tell him how she wrecked my friendship with Eddie, always trying to make me feel too *adult* for him: getting my driver's license, getting good grades, getting engaged, getting a hall for our wedding reception with roast beef and mostaccioli and a band that played Sinatra to Santana.

"I was on my hands and knees," I said. "That's how hard she kicked me. Then gets in her car and dri-i-ives away."

But he just kept stirring and said, "Well, you two will patch it up, I'm sure. You always do."

"Hey, I don't *want* to patch it up. You should have seen her at the wake, Sam. God, you would've —"

"Len."

"What."

"I don't want to hear all this, okay?" He brought the pan and spoon over. "Let's just have a nice, quiet, peaceful dinner." He slid a pile of grey goop onto one of the plates, a pile onto the other, and took the pan to the sink. "Water, milk or beer," he said.

"Neither." I sat down, feeling mad. I didn't usually dump my troubles on Sam but the one time I did I felt like he could at least be a listener. I listened to *his* troubles enough through the years, believe me.

Then, all during the meal, he kept making boring small-talk, stuff like the bus to work being very unreliable, and even about the weather, what a warm early spring we were having, and how was school, and where'd I get the necktie. And he seemed to be enjoying his chicken chow mein about as much as I was, but he kept on eating it, like a job. I mostly just moved mine around.

Then afterwards, doing the dishes, when he asked me about the Blackhawks, I finally said to him, "Sam, cut it out."

"What."

"The way you're talking. You know?"

He knew. He held a soapy plate under the faucet. "Sorry," he said. "Guess I can't think of much to say."

I wasn't sure if he meant he couldn't think of much to say about Eddie being dead, comforting stuff and such, or if he meant he didn't have much to say about *any*thing.

We finished the dishes without talking anymore at all. Then he got a couple of beers out and we brought them into the living room. I took the sofa chair. Sam picked up the book on the couch where I'd left it, and looked at me.

"I was reading it again," I told him.

He tossed it to me.

"I liked it this time, so far," I said.

"Good." He turned on the television and moved the screen about halfway between us. "How's that."

I shrugged.

He moved it more.

"It's fine, Sam."

Bob Newhart was arguing with his wife.

Sam laid on his back along the couch with a little pillow behind his head and put his feet up on the coffee table, holding his beer on his stomach.

I didn't want to watch TV. I didn't know what I wanted, but I didn't want to watch TV.

Bob Newhart's wife said something that cracked up the audience. I glanced at Sam. He could have been staring at a test pattern.

This was the guy, by the way, who used to go on all the time about television-watching, how it's turning everyone into idiots. "Public enemy number one" he always called it.

I started flipping through the pages of my book in a very exaggerated way, like I was looking for something. "What's this guy's name again?" I said, though I knew.

"Bob Newhart," he answered.

"In the *book*, Sam."

He looked at me. "What?"

To hell with this, I decided. "I'm gonna go," I said, and got up. "Let me use your phone."

Sam turned off the TV with his foot and sat up. "Finish your beer first," he said.

I picked it up from the lamp table and tried to drink the whole damn can of it down. I got about halfway.

"Len . . . "

I finished coughing. "What."

"Sit down, will you?"

"I'm fine right here," I told him. "What'd you want?"

"Just sit down, Len. Please."

I gave a big sigh and sat down.

He fished out a cigarette from a pack in his shirt pocket.

"Guess this was a pretty rough day for you, huh?" he said, not looking at me.

I just shrugged. I didn't feel like helping him.

He lit his cigarette and started right away tapping it over the ash tray, nodding.

I waited.

"Listen . . . let me just use the bathroom," he said, and got up and headed there with his cigarette.

I knew he just wanted to get away so he could think of some right things to say to me and then let me leave and he could go back to his TV in peace.

I sat there sipping the rest of my beer. I was going to tell him when he got back to go ahead and catch the rest of Newhart, goodbye, and not even call for a ride but *walk* home. Maybe I'd run into my buddy in the bowling jacket again. I'd say to him, "Fuck you, go ahead," and see if it *was* a gun.

I finished my beer and Sam was still in the bathroom — possibly sitting there getting rid of his chow mein, but I pictured him walking back and forth sucking a cigarette, putting his words together.

And I started feeling bad for him. I mean, after all the different directions he'd gone, ending up here, with nothing to say. Watching television.

Then I got an idea. It was pretty wild but I liked it a lot. I sat up straight and waited for him.

I finally heard the toilet flush, but I knew that trick.

He came back to the couch doing a funeral speech about Eddie. He said he never really knew him but always felt he was a *gentle* person, and probably not as retarded as people thought he was. "Didn't he do a lot of imitations?"

"Sam, listen," I said.

He nodded, listening, pulling out another cigarette.

"Let's leave," I said.

"Well . . . what'd you have in mind? It's getting kind of late."

"No, I mean let's just really *leave*, Sam. You know? Take off. Hit the road. Gone."

"Len . . . "

"I've got about two hundred dollars now, after that hockey stuff I sold, and you've got more than that, right? How much you got?"

"Two hundred and thirty-five dollars, which is in the bank, and that's where it's staying."

"What time's the bank open?"

He sighed.

"No, listen," I said, "this is good. We'll get your money out tomorrow morning and I'll get mine and we'll pack some clothes and head for the hills."

"The hills."

"We'll get jobs here and there, work for a while and move on. You and me, Sam. The Rossini brothers. How about it?"

"Len, listen. I know you're feeling bad about Eddie, and I know —"

"You could keep a journal," I said, pointing at him. "All the ups, the downs. Make a hell of a book."

"I think it's been done."

"Sam, come on with me," I said. "Get out of this. You don't want to watch TV. You know?"

"I thought you were getting married," he said.

"Well, I'm not."

"What about school? I thought you wanted to be a marine biologist."

"And a hockey player and a cowboy."

Sam shook his head. "I'm sorry, Len, but this isn't even worth discussing." He was about to flip the TV on again but I quickly said, "Well, what about *your* little trip?"

That got his attention.

"What about it," he said.

"I'm just saying, you did the same thing."

He nodded. "That's right. Which is why I know what a stupid fucking idea this is, okay?"

"How come you never talk about it?" I asked, before he could get the TV on.

"Because there's nothing to talk *about*," he said. "I went, I came back, and now I'm here. And if *you* go? All you're gonna end up doing is getting lost, in every sense of the word."

Which was kind of what I wanted. "How far did you get?" I asked. "You can tell me that much."

"I don't even know. Missouri somewhere."

"Missouri," I said, keeping him from the TV switch. "That's pretty good, Sam."

"Thanks," he said, sarcastic.

"No, really. Missouri. What was it like there?"

"Bizarre, Len."

"How do you mean? Describe."

"Well, for example, all the convenience stores, instead of being called the White Hen, or Mini-Mart, were called something entirely different," he said. Still being sarcastic.

I said, "No, come on."

"Len, there wasn't anything out there, except my same old stupid goddam self. And after a while —" he shook his head " — I wasn't even sure about *that*."

"How do you mean?"

"I don't know. Let's just drop it, all right?"

"No, go ahead." I could tell he kind of wanted to. "Come on," I said.

He gave a giant sigh. "All I know is, after about three days I started telling everyone who picked me up what my full name was, the town I was from, I have a younger brother named Len, my father's a welder, his name is Lou, my mother's name is Rose, my brother's goldfish are named —"

"Naww."

"All right, but you get the idea."

"Well . . . you missed everybody."

He shook his head. "No. It wasn't that. Hell, I was only out there a week."

"You could still —"

"And then — here's the thing. I started telling this one guy my name was Bob Jones or something, from Milwaukee, Wisconsin. Just to see, right? Bob Jones from Milwaukee, on my way to Mexico City to visit Uncle Pedro on my mother's side. And he bought it. So I told him more. I had a ballerina sister, I think I named her Linda, and a brother in jail —"

"Thanks."

" — and I helped my father run a little butcher shop, and no matter what I said he kept buying it, completely."

"Well, why wouldn't he? You could've been *any*body."

"That's what I'm saying! That's exactly what I'm saying! You know?"

I couldn't say I did. "And so . . . that's why you came back?"

"It was getting *scary*, all right? I'm a chickenshit. We already know that."

"I wasn't saying —"

"I walked across the road and put out my thumb in the other direction and right away I was fine, no problem, I knew exactly who the fuck I was." He stabbed his cigarette into the ash tray and twisted it in with his thumb.

The phone rang.

"Get that," he said, "it's probably Boris." His name for Doris.

It probably was. We both let it ring. Sam flipped open the *TV Guide* on the coffee table. I thumbed the pages of my book, wishing her well. It finally stopped ringing.

"You still taking off?" Sam said, meaning after what he'd told me about *his* trip.

I said I was, yes. "You coming?" I asked.

He didn't even answer. He turned the TV on, changed the channel, and laid back down like he was before.

I said to him, "Sam, it wouldn't be like that with you and

me out there."

He stared at the screen.

"You know?"

He wouldn't answer.

"Sam?"

I gave up.

I decided to get going. I had to pack some clothes and stuff for the morning, plus tell my folks — get *that* over with. But I just kept sitting there staring at the screen along with Sam, not staying or leaving. It was some cop movie. I ended up watching the whole stupid thing. Sam kept falling asleep and waking up, without asking what he'd missed.

Anyway, I spent the night. Sam pulled the coffee table away and opened the little couch into a little bed and laid a blanket and pillow on the floor at the foot of it. He told me I could have the bed. I wasn't sure if he wanted me to accept or not, but I needed the sleep for tomorrow, so I told him thanks.

He said he was setting his alarm clock for eight and was that all right? Was that early enough for my first class?

I said, "Nice try."

"Len . . . "

"What."

"Never mind," he said. "What the fuck do I care?"

After we were both settled in, lights off, I told him I'd send him a postcard from Barcelona.

"Spain," he said. "Interesting choice."

I thought it was in Mexico. "Well, goodnight," I said.

"'night."

I laid there.

After a little while Sam began grinding his teeth, meaning he was asleep. Me, I wasn't even close. For one thing, his bed was like laying on a big bag of toys. But also, the whole idea of heading for the hills in the morning was beginning to seem a little crazy. I started thinking about details, like where would I go, and what would I do when I got there. And actually, all I really *wanted* to be doing was laying somewhere with Doris, with my head on her little white boobs and her hands in my hair while she told me all about how nice I was, what a truly good person I was. Except, I knew Eddie would be there too, his ghost or whatever, disagreeing completely.

Sam said something in his sleep.

I said, "What?"

He didn't answer.

I tried laying on my stomach, on my side, on my back, on my other side, on my stomach again, and about the twenty-fifth time around I fell asleep.

I was standing over Eddie's casket. His eyes were open, looking up at me. I said to him, "Eddie, I'm sorry I quit coming around."

He said, "Eddie, I'm sorry I quit coming around."

I said, "No, listen, okay?"

He said, "No, listen, okay?"

I said, "Eddie, please just listen?"

He said, "Eddie, please just listen?"

I started crying. "Cut it out!" I said.

He started crying. "Cut it out!"

I said, "Eddie!"

He said, "Eddie!"

Then Sam was there, in the dream, trying to drag me away from the casket, but I didn't want to leave and kept pulling my arm back . . . and I woke up crying, Sam shaking my arm in the dark. "Wake up!" he kept saying. "Wake up, dammit."

I lifted my head and yelled, "I *am* awake!" and dumped my face in the pillow again and went on crying.

"Well, quit it then, will you?" he said.

"*No!*" I said, because I knew all over again Eddie was dead and I couldn't stand it.

I kept on crying for quite a while. I wasn't hearing anything more from Sam, and I thought he'd gone back to his blanket. But he hadn't, because all of a sudden here was his *hand* on my back. He still didn't say anything. He just stood there leaning over in the dark, holding his hand on my back.

I started winding down, embarrassment taking over more and more. And by the time I stopped, I just wanted both of us to be asleep again as quick as possible. That's all I wanted. But Sam still had his hand on my back.

"Bad dream," I told him. "Snakes," I said. "They're gone now." I waited. "Sam? Okay?"

He finally spoke. "Okay," he said, real quiet, and took away his hand and went back to his blanket on the floor.

"Well," I said, real loud and breezy, "goodnight!"

"Goodnight," he said, quiet.

I laid there, wide awake all over again.

Sam too, because after a while I heard him go fumbling around for his cigarettes and come back to his blanket and light one up.

We both kept laying there in the dark not saying anything.

I tried telling myself, *You are sleepy . . . you are sleepy . . . you are so, so sleepy . . .*

After a while I heard Sam light another cigarette.

Then I tried remembering the name of every single goldfish I ever had, starting all the way back with Mary and Bill *. . . then Peggy . . . Bigmouth . . . Gabriel . . . Troublemaker . . . Blackspot . . . Maxine . . . .*

The sun was up, filling the kitchen. Sam set down his coffee cup and told Len, still in bed, that he was through now with *verbal* persuasion, and got up from the table.

"Ten minutes," Len promised from under the covers.

"Sorry, kid," said Sam, stepping to the bed, "let's go," and he yanked the blanket away.

"Put it *back*," Len demanded, and drew his knees up closer.

"Get up," Sam told him, "come on. We got a hundred things to do."

"Put the blanket back."

"Len, come on — the *Rossini* brothers, remember? You and me. Sarge and the kid. Come on. Let's go see what's out there."

"Put it back, Sam. Please?"

Sam sighed. "I hate to do this, I really do." He reached down and grabbed his brother by the ankles.

"Don't! Sam! Dammit!"

And by noon they were finally out there, on the side of the bright windy highway — Sam with his thumb out, talking loud about places and possibilities, while Len sat on a suitcase eating an apple in small, thoughtful bites.